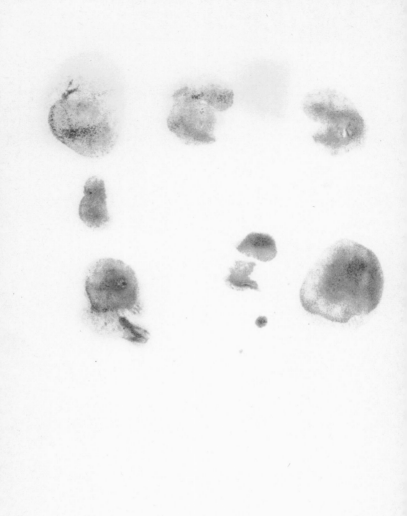

# AGENTS AND PATIENTS

BOOKS BY
# ANTHONY POWELL

NOVELS
*Afternoon Men*
*Venusberg*
*From a View to a Death*
*Agents and Patients*
*What's Become of Waring*

A DANCE TO THE MUSIC OF TIME
*A Question of Upbringing*
*A Buyer's Market*
*The Acceptance World*
*At Lady Molly's*
*Casanova's Chinese Restaurant*
*The Kindly Ones*
*The Valley of Bones*
*The Soldier's Art*
*The Military Philosophers*
*Books Do Furnish a Room*
*Temporary Kings*
*Hearing Secret Harmonies*

BIOGRAPHIES
*John Aubrey and his Friends*

PLAYS
*The Garden God* and *The Rest I'll Whistle*

MEMOIRS
To Keep the Ball Rolling
*Vol. I Infants of the Spring*
*Vol. II. Messengers of Day*

# AGENTS AND PATIENTS

*by*
ANTHONY POWELL

HEINEMANN : LONDON

William Heinemann Ltd
15 Queen Street, Mayfair, London, W1X 8BE

LONDON MELBOURNE TORONTO
JOHANNESBURG AUCKLAND

100979892

FIRST PUBLISHED 1936 (DUCKWORTH)
REPRINTED 1955, 1966, 1973, 1978

434 59902 6

Printed Offset Litho and bound in Great Britain
by Cox & Wyman Ltd,
London, Fakenham and Reading

*For*
*VIOLET GEORGIANA*

'*So in every possible case; He that is not free is not an Agent, but a Patient.*'

WESLEY: Sermon lxvii.

# I

CHIPCHASE, judging it prudent, from an increasingly set expression on Maltravers's face, to bring the story of his emotional life to an end, said:

'I don't pretend that my love affairs are not sordid. They are. They always have been. I like sordid affairs. What I object to is the assumption that just because one's love affairs are sordid it doesn't matter whether or not they go wrong.'

Maltravers said: 'Naturally, naturally. It's far worse. People who have unsordid love affairs have extraneous things to fall back on. Sordid love affairs have to be their own reward.'

After he had said that Maltravers leant forward in the direction of his coffee, stiffly, because his movements were circumscribed by the heavy overcoat he had not removed in spite of the comparative heat of the room. He said:

'The handicaps that I myself have had to contend with in life have been enormous. Simply enormous. But I have come through. I am at one with myself. For example, I don't want money any longer.'

They sat in a high narrow room crowded with chairs and small tables where men and a few women came to drink coffee in sober surroundings. A pleated red curtain, set a foot or two back from the plate glass and rising to half the height of the window, gave the exterior of this coffee-room the appearance of a tailor's shop. The uncurtained window at the back of the room looked out on to a whitewashed wall, so close that even on fine days the place was in twilight. When there was a fog about, the inside, only brightened by the reflections of the gas fire on the metal of the massive funereal urns in which the chicory stewed, was like a cave; and the linoleum floor a vein of grey-pink rock, some volcanic substratum. The time was nearly half-past three in the afternoon and Maltravers and Chipchase had the room to themselves.

When Maltravers talked like this Chipchase knew that he was hard up. Chipchase had suspected this during lunch and now he felt sure of it. Both of them were post-war types, already perhaps a little dated. This was more immediately apparent in the case of Chipchase, whose emaciated physique and severe expression gave some indication of his historical background. He was an art critic by profession and an amateur of psycho-analysis. Maltravers, who was tall and in a genial way distinguished-looking, had connections with the film industry and might have been a better-class gangster figure of any period. The black-and-brown check pattern of his overcoat, the thick striped scarf wound round his neck, and the cloth cap he wore recalled indistinctly an owner-driver of the early days of motoring. They gave no hint of intellectual aptitudes.

Chipchase said: 'When do you go to Berlin?'

'Not for some months. It may even fall through. Meanwhile my Hollywood intrigues continue.'

'I may be crossing the Atlantic in the autumn myself.'

'A lecture tour?'

'On sub-normal psychology. But that may fall through too.'

'What I need,' Maltravers said, 'is new and vital experience. As when I sold religious books from door to door to atone for having lost all my savings gambling with stocks and shares.'

'Why not sell them again?'

2

'It would lose its virtue by repetition.'

'Pay me to put you right psychologically. I share none of your feelings about not wanting money, and you obviously need treatment.'

'Too late.'

Chipchase nodded several times to himself. Since Maltravers had left the government office in which he had begun his career he had had several professions. The most substantial of these had been his film work. He wrote dialogue and adapted scenarios. Like Chipchase he too had dabbled in journalism, which had left both of them with its attendant paranoiac leanings. Chipchase had published a short book on psycho-analysis in relation to automatic writing, but its sales had not been large and it looked as if his life work was to be writing weekly articles on the galleries for a respectable provincial paper. This had been a bad year. Both he and Maltravers were feeling the effects of the trade depression which had set in.

Maltravers drank off his coffee at a gulp.

'When I find a rich man to put up the money for my film,' he said, 'I will employ you.'

'Thank you. As an actor?'

'In a sense. Since you say that you need money.'

'What *I* really want,' Chipchase said, 'is a suitable patient to experiment on for a new system of psychological and psycho-analytical treatment that I am developing. Why not pay me to begin on you?'

'It is in your capacity as psycho-analyst that I should need you if I wanted you at all. I want my film to be a document of behaviour founded to a considerable extent on the findings of psycho-analysis. I take a small group of people. I show certain salient features of themselves. Dreams. Desires. I illustrate their behaviour.'

Chipchase coughed.

'I see,' he said.

'Now you must have noticed,' Maltravers said, 'that a great many of the best films are pictures in which professional actors play minor roles or no role at all. Russian peasants acting Russian peasants. Chinese looking oriental. Children being childish. It's by now a recognised system. My extension of it is to collect a cast of, let us say, intellectuals without previous training and watch them behave intellectually. All I need is a little backing.'

'There must be a great many rich men who would be only too glad to lose a few thousands in that way.'

'You like the idea?'

'Very much. It would fit in well with my own ambitions. If I could find my patient and you your backer we should work excellently in unison. We might even make some money.'

'That,' said Maltravers, 'would be a purely secondary consideration. But think of what tremendous use to the human race a film of such a kind would be.'

'What about Schlumbermayer?'

'Schlumbermayer would not do. Besides, he is not nearly rich enough.'

'Come, come,' Chipchase said.

They paid, left the coffee-room, and began to walk up the street. Maltravers took long swinging strides as if he were trying to shake himself free from his overcoat. Chipchase, in a black hat and carrying a rolled umbrella, hurried along beside him, blown about like an autumn leaf. On the whole the fog had lifted in this part of London, but it hung about in wisps here and there like weeks-old poison gas. The bitter wind scraped agonisingly against their faces. The street ended in an open space and in the south-east corner people had collected to watch certain mysteries which were being enacted there. Maltravers and Chipchase joined

4

the crowd and saw that a man in chains was lying on the ground. Nothing about the day could be said to recommend his dress and his position. He was almost blue-coloured from the cold. Above him stood another man holding a sword.

'What a grand couple,' said Maltravers.

Chipchase stood on tiptoe to see over the shoulder of an elderly negro in spats and a brown bowler hat who was obscuring his view of the performance.

'This is magnificent,' Maltravers said.

The rectangle in which they stood, enclosed on one side by the back of a theatre and on another by red-brick tenement buildings with asphalt courtyards between them, had small shops which sold sweets and groceries and newspapers on the remaining two sides, fronted with posters along their upper storeys. Passages and narrow streets intersected these last blocks of houses. A number of dissociated objects collected together in the middle of the square supplied a surrealist background to the various performers who paused in this place to do their stuff. These objects also added notably to the claustrophobia already induced by the disproportionate height of the surrounding buildings. In the centre of the open space a pile of stones lay beside a wigwam in which a man sat all day long, awaiting the completion of some unachievable labours on the cobbles. Behind him was a small palisade by which a few cars had been parked unevenly and beyond these rested ornate pieces of scenery depicting the sea, delayed in their removal through the back entrance of the theatre. The rectangle was divided in such a way that its four corners were made individual entities in each of which widely opposed activities could be pursued without disturbing one another.

At the moment the man with the sword and his colleague,

gagged and handcuffed on the ground, had attracted the bulk of the crowd. In the north-west corner the Hindu with the tripod, attempting to sell an ointment of his own invention for the cure of cutaneous diseases, had only two young men, his *claque,* listening to him. Even these seemed to have heard his speech so often on past occasions that the words held no longer any magic for them. They stood watching his agitated gestures without attention, sagging forward in their mauve overcoats.

'Rousseau was right,' Chipchase said, 'as regards chains.'

Maltravers said: 'It certainly looks as if nothing in life would sever the one that is round him now.'

Blore-Smith, on his way home from the City, where he had lunched with his solicitor, was already one of the audience. He stood on the other side of the ring of people, opposite Maltravers and Chipchase, whom he did not know, although he noticed and admired Maltravers's overcoat. He was a slightly Jewish-looking young man with huge ears and an impediment in his speech, who had come down from Oxford at the end of the previous summer term and whose big brown eyes and shapeless face still suggested an undergraduate. At present he was reading for the Bar, but he was not much interested in law and did it to have something definite to tell people when they questioned him about himself. He had few friends in London, and when he was not at his crammer's nor in the courts, listening to cases which he hoped would teach him about life, he wandered along the streets, sometimes going into art galleries or cinemas. Entertainments like the one he was witnessing at the moment were a great help in getting him through the day.

The man with the sword, an ape-like primeval character, stripped to the waist and tattooed intermittently, came deliberately towards the fair man lying on the ground and prodded him. The sword was an unimpressive weapon for use with court dress and the ape-man inserted it carefully between the coils of chain with which the fair man's body was gallooned. The chains had made dark marks on the fair man's arms and back, noticeable when he writhed and dragged up the vest he wore, showing the flesh beneath. The man with the sword was an athletic type with black hair growing low on his forehead and a sore on his face. He continued to prod, muttering all the time to himself. Then he turned unexpectedly, startling almost to flight Blore-Smith, who was standing nearest to him, and shouted as loudly as possible and as if overcome with disgust and loathing for the spectators:

'Can't you see what the poor chap's suffering? Aren't there any sportsmen here? What's the good of one-and-a-tanner?'

Response to this appeal was not immediate. Blore-Smith, although he had already contributed sixpence, would have given something more if he had not been so embarrassingly close. The ape-man, exasperated, threw the sword on the ground and, grinding his teeth, walked slowly to the other side of the open space, where a dilapidated small car stood by the tenements. Putting his hand under the number-plate, he lifted this from behind and shook it so that the car rattled and showed signs of dissolution.

Maltravers left Chipchase on the outskirts of the crowd behind the negro and pushed his way to the front row, where he stood among a group of small children, some of whom watched the show while others fought among themselves.

The ape-man returned from shaking the car. He picked up the sword from the ground and leant over the other man. While he did this he rolled his eyes in a paroxysm of fury. He said:

'You tied me up in Piccadilly and left me there for three hours, did you? Well, now you're going to see what it's like.'

Turning again to the crowd, he said:

'Come on, isn't there a gent among the lot of you to give a poor fellow more than one and eightpence? Why, I've been doing this turn for fifteen years and if it wasn't a fine decent entertainment would I be doing it to this day, I ask you, ladies and gentlemen?'

He showed his teeth. There were flecks of grey foam round his mouth. A girl watching from the first-floor window of one of the sweet shops threw a penny that rolled up to his feet.

'Thank you, missy, thank you.'

The ash-blonde who had thrown the coin smiled and swallowed shyly to herself. A car passed, slowing up to avoid running over the man in fetters. The man with the sword made towards it savagely as if he were going to seize it by the footboard and overturn it by force. Changing his mind, however, he allowed it to pass. The man in fetters struggled to his knees. For a time he rocked from side to side. A board with spikes in it was strapped firmly to his back.

Maltravers, watching with interest, began to unbutton his overcoat. Feeling in his trouser pocket, he found five coppers and threw them to the man with the sword. He threw them singly and slowly—one—two—three—four—five.

'Thank you, sir, thank you.'

The ape-man now passed the sword through the elbows of the other so that the flat of the blade pressed against his back. The fair man began to groan and to struggle violently as if he were on the point of having a fit. His position and gestures recalled some high-renaissance picture of Jacob

8

wrestling with the Angel in which the Angel is not pictorially represented, being suggested only by the contortions of Jacob. After a time the fair man freed his arms from the chains and threw aside the spiked board. Then he loosened the gag and spat it out on to the cobbles. He stood squirming with the handcuffs. The ape-man said sternly:

'At the close of this remarkable exhibition my friend will oblige with a display of eating coal and candles.'

He put down the sword among a heap of assorted instruments of torture, which with his coat and hat lay on a piece of newspaper, and picking up a comb he began to tidy his hair. Chipchase, who had a bad circulation, was getting chilly, and he entered the crowd in search of Maltravers. Stepping over one of the smaller children who had fallen to the ground, he said:

'Shall we go? I don't think this is so good a show as the organ and the transvest male dancers.'

'It has its points.'

'Well, I'm off.'

'All right, I'll come too. Do you want a lift?'

'Which way are you going?'

'Home.'

'No,' said Chipchase. 'You're no good to me in that case. I've got to cover a show at the Frott Gallery. I missed the private view.'

They went off together towards the side street where Maltravers had parked his car, a torpedo-shaped gamboge machine bought second-hand from the editor of a motor paper. Tuned-up, she was rumoured to do eighty-seven. Maltravers climbed up and stepped in to avoid opening the door.

'Give Reggie my love,' he said.

'And mine to Sarah.'

Maltravers waved his hand and drove away. Chipchase turned up his coat-collar and slunk off, keeping close to the walls of the houses to avoid the wind.

Blore-Smith, having nothing better to do, stayed to watch the candle-eating. He was an unexceptional young man whose head was too large for his body. The lower grades of the civil service or an assistant mastership at a public school would have provided a suitable role for him. Both his parents, Midland business people, had died when he was a child, and on coming of age he had inherited an income of several thousands a year, so that he was faced with the task of finding an occupation more in keeping than these with his station in life. His guardian had insisted on a short allowance at the university during his minority, with the result that Blore-Smith had made fewer friends than might otherwise have been the case. His own temperament had caused him to choose these few friends from the dullest circles available during his residence. Life at Oxford had been lonely and obscure, but his solitude and a lack of distinction did not become apparent to him until he had lived for some months in London. At the same time he preferred London. It was bigger and there were more cinemas. Sometimes he went to see his sister, older than himself and married to a nose specialist, or he attended dinner-parties given by people who had known his family. These made a change, but they did not constitute much of a framework for the adult life which he had supposed that he would lead when finished with his education. The young men whom he met on these occasions led compact, hearty little lives of their own and the girls were bouncing or half-baked. Blore-Smith had even hoped on coming down from Oxford that he would have opportunities for friendship with the opposite sex. But although in London this was not openly put a stop to by the authorities it seemed no less difficult to achieve. He kept up with some of his Oxford friends. Secretly he had begun to look upon them as a grim crowd, now that they appeared in the chiaroscuro of London, unrelieved by a background of dreaming spires, and lately he had seen less and less of them. A great deal of his time was spent in his room reading, or looking at the illustrated papers at the Royal Automobile Club, for which his brother-in-law had put him up. His comparative affluence seemed no help. In the first place he disliked the idea of spending a lot of money all at once, and in the second he could think of nothing that he wanted to spend it on which would not complicate life in a way which alarmed him. He took rooms in Ebury Street because he had heard of it as a place where bachelors lived, and, although he managed to pay about double their market value, his income was still far in advance of what he needed. He was interested in a rather pedantic way in contemporary art and letters and he had sometimes considered making a collection of modern pictures or even, in his wilder moments, founding a magazine. He could never bring himself to lay the foundations of the former hobby and the latter he knew to be a purely romantic conception, because he had no idea what the magazine would be about nor who would write in it. A larger establishment would involve dealing with servants; he was unable to distinguish one make of car from another and he knew only too well that he would never be able to drive one; wearing new clothes made him feel embarrassed; expensive restaurants were not places to go to alone; he had once got drunk at a Bump Supper and had scarcely tasted alcohol since; he never lent money to his friends because he had once been told that to lend money to a friend was a sure way to lose him, and although he now, in fact, wanted to lose his present friends, a system of multiple loans seemed the least advantageous method of setting about it. All the more obvious ways of getting rid of increment were therefore closed to him and his money remained on deposit account at the bank. Blore-Smith knew that there was a good deal to be said for this, but at the same time he was dissatisfied. Life showed every sign of being a disappointment.

It was because of this consistent lack of incident in his day that Blore-Smith was so absorbed by the candle-eating. On the whole this was a success and it was followed by the swallowing of fire and lighted cigarettes. After a while, like all things good and bad, the display came to an end. The crowd dispersed. Blore-Smith walked away, ruminating on what he had seen. It had given him food for thought. He too felt himself chained. Chained by circumstance. Again he toyed in his mind with the idea of collecting hour-glasses or first editions or something of the sort. He knew that a little decision was all that was necessary. But steps of that kind needed a command of initiative. He decided that at least he would drop in to an art gallery before it was time to go home and have another go at Cheshire's *Modern Real Property*.

Maltravers drove north in the direction of his flat. He went through Bloomsbury and soon he had passed the gothic spires of some railway station and was driving along grey steep roads that led uphill. While he jarred his wheels over the tram-lines he thought about the interlude that he and Chipchase had seen performed in the space beside the tenements. He wondered whether he could get from it any ideas that might prolong his connection with the film trade. From practical matters he moved on to the scene's symbolic aspects. Like Blore-Smith, he had been impressed by these.

They were several in number and he gave careful consideration to all of them.

In this part of London the light was always of a thin quality and passing through its streets gave the illusion of cinema. The wind swept by him down the hill and blew noisily through the exhibits outside the shop where they sold tombstones. Maltravers glanced in the direction of the memorials in this yard, as he did whenever he went by it, to remind himself of man's impermanence. On the right was the green embankment of the reservoir and later the statue of Sir Hugh Myddelton. He turned off down a lane that led to a wide treeless square and stopping in front of one of the houses at the far end he opened the door and went up the stairs to the top floor. In the sitting-room Sarah stood by the window, eating a slice of bread spread with Gentleman's Relish and holding a cup in her hand.

There were two or three tables in the room, littered with sheets of foolscap, books and tea-things. On one of these were three typewriters and on another a gramophone. A number of newspapers lay about, some of which had been crumpled up and left on the floor. A wide sofa stood in front of the fire, also covered with typescript and books, while the two arm-chairs were piled high with gramophone records. The two remaining chairs were chromium-plated and had no back legs, the seats being supported by the front legs alone which curved back and united below them. Press-cuttings, invitations, and snapshots were stuck in the sides of the gilt empire mirror which hung over the mantelpiece.

Stepping over two cats and paying no attention to Sarah, Maltravers walked across the room. Without taking off his cap he went to one of the typewriters and sat down at it with his feet stretched out in front of him. Then he sighed and began to type. Sarah finished her bread and Gentleman's Relish. She put down her cup on the gramophone and said:

'Do you want some tea?'

'No.'

'What sort of a day have you had?'

Maltravers did not answer. He gritted his teeth and went on typing. Sarah poured out for herself another cup of tea. She said:

'Did you lunch with Oliver?'

'Yes,' said Maltravers, making no secret of the effort it was for him at that moment to answer questions.

'How was he?'

'I had to listen to a lot of stuff about his girl.'

'Poor dear.'

'Him or her or me?'

'All of you.'

Maltravers grunted. Then he sniffed several times and began to type away again. While he did this he listened to Sarah gulping her tea. Nearly a minute passed before she said:

'I'm going out tonight.'

Maltravers jumped up from the chromium-plated chair, tore the sheet of paper out of the typewriter, crushed it in his hand, and threw it into the waste-paper basket. He said:

'Why can't I ever have two minutes' peace? Must I be bothered every moment of the day and night by you and your incessant chattering?'

'I only said that I was going out.'

'Well, what of it? I don't care. What business is it of mine? I don't mind whom you go out with. You always talk as if you were going to run away with someone.'

'I probably am.'

'Well, what do you expect me to do about it?'

'I thought you might like to have some warning.'

Maltravers took off his cap and threw it on the table. It fell with its peak in the butter. He said:

'This afternoon I watched a man with a sword who was prodding another man who was gagged and chained and lying on the ground. That's what I feel like in our married life. I lie on the ground gagged and chained and you prod me with a sword.'

'Where on earth did you see all these extraordinary things happening?'

'Who are you going out with tonight?'

'I don't expect it would interest you.'

'It doesn't interest me. I'm ordering you to tell me.'

'I don't see why I should.'

'I'm your husband.'

'You seldom treat me like a wife.'

'Who is it?'

'I shan't tell you.'

'Who is it? Come on now.'

'It's Nipper, if you really want to know.'

Maltravers sat down heavily on the chair, which vibrated beneath him.

'Heavens above,' he said. 'Heavens above.'

Sarah began to clear up the tea-things.

'Shall I leave the tea?' she said, 'or shall I put the kettle on and make you some more?'

Maltravers said: 'It's not that I mind. I don't care who you make friends with. Zulus, condemned criminals, Scotch nationalists, they'd all be the same to me. It's only that I can't conceal my surprise that you should be able, far less choose, to spend a single moment more than necessary with a creature like Nipper.'

He stared hard at Sarah, who stood beside the wireless set, holding a teapot and watching him, but showing no interest in what he was saying. She said:

'You've only met Nipper once and then he was in fancy dress, wearing a mask.'

'That was enough for me. God forbid that I should ever spend any time in his company when he's not wearing one.'

'Anyway, it's me that's going out with him tonight, not you.'

'You can't go.'

'What do you mean?'

'I forbid you to go.'

'You—forbid—me—to—go?'

Sarah began to roar with laughter. She repeated the phrase several times. Maltravers turned away from her and occupied himself with his typewriter, inserting another sheet of foolscap. Sarah put down the kettle for a second and lit a cigarette with a spill. Then she went out of the sitting-room and the noises of washing-up came from the kitchen. Maltravers concentrated on the scenario he was mapping out. The two cats who until now had been asleep rose simultaneously and pompously made for the door. Maltravers let them out and sat for some time, brooding in front of the typewriter, sometimes tapping out a few sentences.

At last he shouted:

'Sarah.'

There was no answer. He shouted again. Nothing happened. He got up and went out into the passage. The noise of running water came from the bathroom. Maltravers went as far as the bathroom door and tried to get in. The door was locked and he hammered on it. From inside the bathroom Sarah said:

'Hullo? What do you want?'

'Is there anything to eat in the house?'

'I can't hear.'

'Is there anything to eat in the house?'

'What?'

'Turn the water off.'

'Now what is it?'

'Is there anything to eat in the house?'

'Yes, lots.'

'What time does Mrs. Doon come back in the evening?'

'You told her we shouldn't want her tonight.'

'Hell!'

'There's lots of cold food. You can easily manage by yourself.'

Maltravers did not answer at once. He was too angry. Sarah turned the water on again and began to sing and splash about. Maltravers, putting his mouth to the crack in the door, said:

'You're a magnificent wife for a man to have, I must say.'

'What?'

'Turn the water off.'

Sarah again stopped the tap running. Maltravers said:

'I only wanted to tell you that I think you are a magnificent wife for a man to have.'

'Well, you were out every day last week.'

'What if I was?'

'Well, it's my turn to go out tonight.'

'When I go out and leave you alone it's because I'm trying to persuade influential people to give me a job. It's not because I want to go to the cinema with a little rat of a man who wears his jumper tucked inside his trousers.'

'Why shouldn't he? It doesn't look half so funny as some of the clothes you wear. Besides, you told me yourself that on Tuesday you gave that beastly Swedish girl dinner and on Wednesday you had dinner with Mendie. I don't suppose you expected to get a job from either of them.'

'Shut up.'

'Go away then and don't disturb me in my bath.'

17

'All right,' said Maltravers, 'I will go away. And it will be some time before you see me again.'

'I don't care.'

Maltravers went back to the sitting-room and put on his overcoat. While he was rubbing the butter off the peak of his cap he heard Sarah calling from the bathroom. He took no notice. After slamming the door of the flat as loudly as possible he went downstairs again and got into the car.

Chipchase continued to walk in the direction of Bond Street. He stopped to look at many shop-windows as he passed, absorbed by money-making phantasies. He varied these with thoughts of Caroline, with whom he had broken off relations finally the night before, tormenting himself with images of his potential successor. Caroline being given a good time by stockbrokers or minor poets; by cads with high-powered motor-cars or rather tousled painters; sitting in the rooms of undergraduates who did not really care for women at all; having dinner with very very old clubmen with complicated desires, refined Americans who played polo, or tanned and stuttering colonial officials home on leave; with intelligent men, with appalling men, or with saintly men who just went about doing good; Guardees and naval officers and secretaries from the Latin-American legations; with Parsee students, White Russians, Jewish actors, or nestling in the arms of some strapping Senegalese. Filled with gloom he reached the doors of the Frott Gallery.

Inside by the entrance was a notice *Catalogues 1s.* and a plate for the money. Chipchase took a catalogue without paying for it and went towards the inner room. Reggie Frott, the owner of the gallery, was standing in the corner talking to a tall man with a curly moustache beginning to go grey, who wore a single eyeglass and leant against the wall with one hand on his hip and an air of an Elder

18

Statesman. Reggie, when he saw Chipchase, came closer to his client and, lowering his head, grimaced diabolically through the space enclosed by the older man's ribs and the flying buttress of his elbow. Chipchase raised his eyebrows and smiled and then moved about the room looking at the pictures, an *avant-garde* selection in which canvas and paint were helped out by the adhesion of small pieces of looking-glass, sea-shells, match-boxes, and newspaper. Touching one of the seascapes with his hand, Chipchase loosened a bead, but found himself able to stick it on again without attracting Reggie's attention. He killed some minutes in this way, making pencil notes in the margin of his catalogue, until the man with the eyeglass had succeeded in edging his way to the door of the gallery and subsequently out into the street without being persuaded to buy the more-than-life-size statue of Pomona, executed in green basalt by a German sculptor, which Reggie was bent on selling him.

Chipchase sat down on the low sofa and waited. Reggie shut the door and ambled across the room again. Reggie that afternoon was looking more than ever himself, an intemperate little boy of twelve years old or, alternatively, an octogenarian jockey left over from the Phil May period, threatening reminiscences of Romano's and the old *Pink 'Un* gang, ageless but at the same time heavily dated. For a time he stood in front of Chipchase, rolling from side to side and belching. At last he said:

'Well, you old swine, how are you?'

'Just ticking over.'

'Do you know what time I got to bed this morning?'

'When?'

'Eight o'clock. And it wasn't my own bed then.'

Reggie put his hands in his pockets, swivelled round on his heel, and began to chant in a tuneless sing-song:

*'Beds—beds—beds—beds—*
*And it wasn't my own bed then.'*

Then he took a small bottle from his pocket and smelt the grey liquid inside.

'Time to take my medicine,' he said. 'Have some?'

'No.'

'Do. It's awfully good for you. Gets rid of all the poison inside.'

'I prefer to keep mine.'

'Just as you like, you old devil.'

Reggie opened a cupboard concealed in the wall and took a tumbler from the shelf inside, where it stood with several other glasses, an empty gin bottle, some aspirin tablets, and a broken piece of negro carving. Putting it on a flattish piece of sculpture resembling a miniature model of the Blarney Stone, he poured out some of the medicine. He said:

'I had a damn good dinner on Schlumbermayer last night. And the best three-shilling cigar in the whole of London.'

He drank off the medicine, gently belched again, and put the glass back into the cupboard. He said:

'And we rounded it off with half a bottle of Napoleon brandy.'

'Did you manage to sell your host anything at the end of it?'

Reggie slipped his arm round the waist of the statue of Pomona. He said:

'He's coming in tomorrow and should buy something really worth while. And, by the way, why weren't you here to write up the private view?'

'I've come to do that now. Is anything selling?'

'Not a thing. Mind you say something polite.'

'They won't print it if I'm too kind. I can't risk losing my job. Money's much too scarce. Who was that you were trying to land Pomona on?'

'Why, Algy Teape, of course. You must know the gallant Colonel Teape?'

'So that's Colonel Teape, is it?'

'One of the best-known faces along the old *Côte d'Azur!*'

'*Ah, oui, oui. Je comprends.*'

'That's just as well for you,' Reggie said. He put his other arm round Pomona's waist and, looking up into her face, said:

'She's an ugly old girl, isn't she?'

'Not my type.'

'The Colonel didn't think she was his either.'

'He's a friend of Pauline de Borodino's, isn't he?'

'Yes. In fact he said that he thought Pomona was more in her line than his.'

'Did he, did he?'

It was at this moment that Blore-Smith came into the gallery. Although he had stayed to watch the candle-eating he walked quicker than Chipchase and he had not delayed his progress by looking into so many shop-windows. He took a catalogue, put a shilling in the plate, and began to inspect the show, beginning at the exhibit marked *No. 1*. Reggie, not seeing him arrive, or seeing and not caring, moved his arms lower down the body of the statue, at the same time retreating his feet so that in a few seconds he had lowered himself on the level of the carpet where he lay with his head resting sideways on Pomona's pedestal. He groaned several times and said:

'What I need is a good lie down.'

'That's exactly what you seem to be having.'

Blore-Smith, out of the corner of his eye, watched the scene nervously, and delayed for several minutes among the smaller pictures to allow Reggie to resume a more conventional posture.

While he was doing this Blore-Smith came to a great decision. He too would break away from the chains that bound him. On that afternoon he would lay the foundation-stone of a more serious life. He would begin to make a collection of modern pictures. Suddenly he saw quite plainly that what he wanted was a hobby. He watched Reggie rise from his knees and light a cigarette.

'What have you the impertinence to ask for this object?' Chipchase said, tapping Pomona on the behind.

Reggie reached for a book that lay on his desk and began to turn over the pages. He said:

'I have to be careful about answering that sort of question. I sometimes get our code muddled up and the other day I sold a picture for eighteen guineas that ought to have been a hundred and eighty. So, you see, I have to be absolutely sure even with an old friend like you.'

Blore-Smith had by now come up quite close and with his back to them stood listening to their conversation. Reggie ran his finger down the page. At last he said:

'To you—and to you only, mark you—we could do this for—let me see—shall we say three hundred guineas?'

'Yes,' said Chipchase, 'let's say that.'

'It's really awfully cheap,' Reggie said. 'It would fetch almost that in Paris.'

'Somebody may buy it.'

'You never can tell,' Reggie said. 'Why, I sold a thing nearly twice that size once for the same amount. It's in a museum now, so, thank goodness, it won't pass through my hands again.'

In the background Blore-Smith was trying to collect all his courage. His mouth had gone dry. His legs shook under him. Clutching his umbrella, he stepped forward awkwardly in the direction of Reggie and said:

'How much is that picture? That one there.'

Reggie shut the price-book with a snap and eyed Blore-Smith disapprovingly. Then he looked him up and down slowly as if he were valuing an unsaleable piece of sculpture.

'What picture?' he said, after he had given Blore-Smith time to flush painfully.

'That one.'

Blore-Smith pointed with his umbrella and accidentally touched one of Pomona's arms.

'Mind,' said Reggie. 'Mind. Don't break the whole place up.'

He went over and had a look at the picture which Blore-Smith had indicated and returned to his book, turning over the pages very deliberately. Blore-Smith leant with all his weight on his umbrella, trying to give himself confidence. Reggie put his head on one side and stuck out his lower lip, a favourite mannerism.

'That's two hundred guineas,' he said.

He shut the book noisily again and glared at Blore-Smith.

'I should like to buy it,' Blore-Smith said. The room went black all round him.

For the moment Reggie was taken off his guard. For a brief second the veil was torn aside and all his knowingness became wide-eyed uncertainty, like a frightened child's. Blore-Smith, now that he had said the words, felt much better. They had acted as a spiritual purge. He stood looking at Reggie quite sternly. Chipchase folded up the catalogue on which he had been making notes and put it into his pocket. He wondered whether Blore-Smith was in full possession of his faculties. It was almost inconceivable that a total stranger both to Reggie and to himself should be prepared to pay two hundred guineas for a picture of that sort. Almost at once Reggie recovered himself and said:

'The frame would, of course, be a little extra. It's a special one, as you see.'

'Naturally.'

'That would only be a matter of a pound or two.'

'Quite.'

'And now,' said Reggie, almost his old self, 'you must give me your name and address, for although I know your face very well and I'm sure we must have met, I can't remember any details. I expect I may have been a bit boiled at the time. Have you got a cheque-book with you? No? Then we have some blank forms here.'

Reggie pulled back the chair at the desk for Blore-Smith to sit on and at the same time handed him a fountain-pen.

'Who shall I make it out to?'

'Well,' said Reggie, 'I should think you might make it payable to R. Orlebar Frott, Esquire'; and turning to Chipchase he added:

'It won't do my private account any harm to have a little money circulating through it again.'

'And how much is the sum exactly?'

'As we haven't had any previous dealings it's customary to pay a third in advance, which would be—let me see——'

'Oh, I'd rather pay the whole lot now.'

Before replying Reggie turned in Chipchase's direction and puffed out his cheeks.

'In that case,' he said, 'that will be two hundred and seventeen pounds, thirteen shillings and ninepence. That will include carriage to within a mile from here.'

'And when shall I get it?'

'The show closes at the end of the month.'

'Will you send it to the Ebury Street address?'

'We'll send it right along.'

Later, Blore-Smith never knew how he got out of the

gallery. He felt faint and his legs seemed about to give way. There was a loud humming in his ears. As he closed the door behind him he could hear Reggie giving peal after peal of laughter. He wondered what he had done that seemed so funny and tried to feel convinced that after all it could not be himself that Reggie was laughing at. He made an effort to pull himself together and concentrated on trying to remember which direction he should take in order to return to his rooms. He was dazed but at the same time rather happy.

'Who was it?' Chipchase said, when Reggie had stopped laughing.

Reggie looked at the address. He said:

'That was Mr. Blore-Smith, that was.'

'He seems anxious to get rid of his money as soon as possible.'

Reggie rubbed his hands together. He said:

'We've got to see if his money is any good first and when we've done that we'll sit back and show him some more pretty pictures.'

'I want to meet a man myself with some money he wants to get rid of.'

'I'll introduce you one of these days.'

'I wish you would.'

'What do you want to do with him, anyway?'

'A little scheme he might be interested in.'

'Something dirty?'

'No,' said Chipchase. 'Something eminently clean. As clean as driven snow. Cleaner if possible.'

Reggie, who had collapsed by now on the sofa, put his feet up and was about to go to sleep again when he was disturbed by the sound of someone coming into the gallery. This time it was a woman. She was tall and fair-haired and wore an overcoat of military cut. As she came in she unbuttoned this and put her hands on her hips, showing a tweed skirt and jumper under her coat. Stepping out like a man, she strode across the floor towards them. Her carriage suggested that she was unable to decide whether she wanted to be taken for a discontented tragedy queen on a holiday or a careless tomboy caught up through no fault of her own in serious bohemian life. Whichever it was, she was unmistakably a beauty. Reggie jumped up from the sofa.

'Mrs. Mendoza!' he said. 'How are you?'

Chipchase stood up too and the woman laughed and kissed both of them. She took off her hat and threw it on to the desk, shaking out her hair.

'How's Mrs. M.?' Chipchase said.

'Pretty bad.'

'What is it this time?'

'Everything. Money chiefly.'

Reggie said: 'I've had a man in here who gave me a cheque for two hundred guineas for one of the worst pictures I have ever hung in my gallery—and between you and me that's saying a good deal. What do you think of that for a business coup, Mendie?'

'Obviously it will turn out to be a dud.'

'He wasn't the sort of young man who gives stumer cheques.'

'What sort of a young man was he?' said Mrs. Mendoza, showing some interest for the first time since she had been in the gallery.

'Well,' said Reggie, turning to Chipchase, 'what sort of a young man was he?'

Chipchase said: 'He looked as if he would do for Mendie very well. He must be over fifteen and he's evidently got some money. He'd be all right if he had his hair cut and changed his tailor and was taught a little about art.'

'You always want everybody's individuality taken away from them,' Mrs. Mendoza said.

'Fortunately this young man hadn't got any.'

'I don't believe you.'

'I see you have fallen for him already.'

'I think he sounds sweet.'

'He is. You'll adore him. Reggie will have to arrange a meeting.'

'What have I got to do?' said Reggie, who was again attempting to go to sleep on the sofa. He groped about with one arm in the air in the direction of Mrs. Mendoza.

'Go to sleep, my pet, that's all you have to do,' she said, patting him on the head.

'How's the flower business, Mendie?' Chipchase said.

'So-so.'

'Don't talk so much,' Reggie said. 'I can't sleep with so much noise going on.'

Mrs. Mendoza pulled his hair. Reggie writhed.

'Don't be so ungrateful,' she said. 'I happened to be passing and out of sheer kindness I came in to relieve your boredom, and all you do is to go to sleep.'

'It was very sweet of you, Mendie darling. Let's all have dinner together?'

'I can't,' said Chipchase. 'I've got a date.'

'Neither can I,' said Mrs. Mendoza. 'I'm dining with the Commodore.'

'Cut him.'

'He'd be furious.'

'He'd get over it.'

'No, he wouldn't.'

'Of course he would.'

'It would spoil his week.'

'He'd forget about it.'

Mrs. Mendoza said: 'An elephant *never* forgets.'

'I must go now,' Chipchase said. 'There are several things I want to do before dinner.'

He got up and walked once round the room to have a last look at the pictures. He was about to leave the gallery when Mrs. Mendoza said:

'Wait a moment. I'll walk with you some of the way.'

'Don't leave me all alone,' Reggie said. 'I can't bear it.'

'You've brought it on yourself,' Chipchase said.

They put an overcoat on top of Reggie and some rugs imported from Paris and left him lying on the sofa. By the time they had reached the door he had begun to snore. After the warmth of the gallery the street seemed cold and dispiriting.

'When is your date?' Mrs. Mendoza said. 'Why not come back to *la cattleya* for a bit?'

'All right.'

After some discussion as to whether they could between them afford a taxi, it was decided that they should walk, and they went along Piccadilly, striking south at Hyde Park Corner and passing through Belgrave Square.

Having no immediate objective ahead of him, Maltravers sat for several minutes in the car in front of his house, reviewing the drawbacks of married life. He had wanted to get some work done that afternoon, but since Sarah had made work impossible there seemed nothing for it but to call on one or another of his friends. That was, if he had any friends. He began to go through the list. There was Griffin Griffiths, but he did not feel altogether in the vein for Griffin Griffiths, who, besides, lived a long way away. Gubbins, three-parts crazy, was always ready for a talk. When Maltravers had last dined with him Gubbins had spent the greater part of dinner trying to balance a loaf of bread on his head. That would be worse than Griffin

Griffiths. Maltravers was in no mood for the repetition of such behaviour tonight. He dismissed all thought of Gubbins from his mind. Chipchase would be somewhere between his flat and the Frott Gallery or prosecuting some depressing love affair away in the suburbs. There was McConochie; Twysleton-Carbery; Schlumbermayer; or Ingrid? And then suddenly Maltravers had a good idea. He would go and see Mrs. Mendoza in her flower-shop. He started up the engine.

Mrs. Mendoza's flower-shop, *la cattleya,* as she had portentously named it, was in the neighbourhood of Sloane Square and about this time of day she was usually at home. Even if she should be out there would be someone left in charge to whom it would be possible to talk. Either Commander Venables, a retired naval admirer of hers, or Scrubb, the medical student who lived in a small flat at the top of the house. Scrubb, when behindhand with his rent, was made to sit for hours together in the shop surrounded by medical books, grudgingly selling flowers to customers who might drop in while Mrs. Mendoza was out with her friends.

Maltravers drove off. He wanted to talk to someone, anyone, as soon as possible. He drove the gamboge car in and out of the traffic, skidding along once more over the tramlines on the way down the hill. The evening light made visibility bad.

It was later, when he had reached the S.W. district, that the accident occurred and then, as it happened, the light had almost nothing to do with it. The fault lay entirely with Blore-Smith, who had walked in a dazed condition all the way from the Frott Gallery, facing death more than once while he did so from lorries and errand-boys on bicycles. Maltravers's speed was excessive, but he knew that his brakes were reliable, so that Blore-Smith's sudden decision to step off the pavement almost under the wheels of the gamboge car found him quite prepared, although Blore-Smith had been standing on the edge of the kerb for several seconds, watching the street and showing only very faint signs of wanting to cross to the far side.

The collision was sufficiently violent to knock Blore-Smith off his feet, but he fell very slowly, landing on his hands and knees, and although covered with mud he was able to get up by his own efforts. Maltravers got out of the car at once and ran round to the front.

'Really that was too bad. I am so very sorry. Let me brush some of that off. It was a most unfortunate thing to have happened.'

Inwardly Maltravers composed a line of attack in case Blore-Smith should turn nasty.

Blore-Smith, still winded, said something about it all being his own fault and not mattering in the least. He picked up his umbrella and tried to get away, but Maltravers, seeing the spirit in which Blore-Smith proposed to accept the accident, took him by the arm.

'You can't possibly go away like this,' he said. 'Why, I've hardly had time to apologise to you at all. You must come and have a drink with me so that I can make some amends for having done this. Are you in a hurry? Are you on your way to an important engagement?'

Blore-Smith was surprised by all this. He was still rather shaken by his picture-buying as well as by his fall. He said:

'I was on my way home.'

'What were you going to do there?'

'What was I going to do?'

'Yes. Had you anything to look forward to?'

'I hardly know. I think I was going to read a little before dinner.'

Still holding his arm, Maltravers led Blore-Smith into the car.

'In that case,' he said, 'you must certainly come and have a drink. It will do your nerves good after the shock they have had. There is a place I know of just round the corner.'

Slipping into reverse, Maltravers shot back the car quickly, throwing Blore-Smith down into the seat, which was low and sloped at so sharp an angle that already he felt almost horizontal to the road. Then they drove rapidly up a side turning and stopped.

'Here we are,' Maltravers said.

It was the first time since he had been in London that Blore-Smith had entered a public-house. He had always imagined that such places were filled with drunken navvies and old women wearing men's caps and smoking clay pipes. It was something of a surprise for him to find himself in a room that reminded him of a seaside tea-shop.

'What will you drink?' Maltravers said.

'Oh, anything.'

'But you must have some preference.'

'Oh, beer, I should think,' said Blore-Smith desperately. He had begun to wonder whether he would ever escape from this man. He still felt a little stunned.

'A pint of bitter and a double White Horse,' Maltravers said. 'Let's sit down by the fire. It's more comfortable.'

Not many people had spoken kindly to Blore-Smith in the course of his life. Incompetence at games had soured his schooldays, causing him to be disliked equally by masters and boys at the small public school to which he had been sent. Although he had come into his money in time for his last term at Oxford and there were those who, if properly approached, might have been prepared at an earlier period to help him enjoy it, his personal appearance and his shyness caused both them and himself to feel that any such opportunity that there might have been had come too late. He had worked hard and had tried to please the dons, but even his tutor could not conceal his conviction that he had a right to expect of his pupils a higher standard of looks than Blore-Smith could offer. In the circumstances Maltravers, who depended on shock-tactics as one of his chief means of earning a livelihood, made a distinctly favourable impression. Soon after the second round Blore-Smith had told him most of his life story, though natural caution made him minimise the extent of his income. Maltravers listened and nodded his head at intervals to show that he understood about all these things.

'What college were you at?' he said.

Blore-Smith told him.

'Yes,' Maltravers said. 'Yes. I knew someone who was there. You've had a hard time.'

'London is such a disappointment,' Blore-Smith said.

He felt that he had now gone so far that he had better tell Maltravers everything. He said:

'One doesn't seem to get any of the things one expected.'

'What sort of things?'

'Well, I mean life and so on.'

'But you seem to get plenty of excitement. For instance, I've just knocked you down in my car.'

'Oh, I don't mean things like that,' Blore-Smith said.

He hesitated.

'Women,' he said, and then he felt that he had gone too far. In fact he saw by Maltravers's face that he had.

'Women?' Maltravers said. 'Women? Why, the whole place teems with them. They're impossible to get away from.'

'Oh, I don't mean tarts.'

'Neither do I. I think it rather insulting of you that you should suggest that I did.'

32

'I'm sorry,' Blore-Smith said, much embarrassed. 'I know I oughn't to have said that. I suppose I really oughtn't to have mentioned the subject to an absolute stranger anyway. But you seemed the first person that I've ever met who understood what I meant when I talked about these things.'

His solicitor had given him a light stand-up lunch and the unaccustomed quart of beer he had just drunk made Blore-Smith feel full of self-pity.

'And besides,' he said, 'I didn't mean only women. I meant life and excitement. Meeting people who count and doing important business.'

'Like one of Balzac's heroes.'

'Yes, I suppose so,' said Blore-Smith, wondering whether he ought to admit that he had never read Balzac.

Maltravers nodded his head slowly.

'Ah-ha,' he said. 'Ah-ha.'

'I'm sure you do all these things,' Blore-Smith said.

By now he was quite breathless.

'Yes,' said Maltravers. 'I do all these things.'

He sat, still wearing his cap and scarf and oppressively big overcoat, and looked hard at Blore-Smith. There was a pause in which Blore-Smith tried to regain some breath. Maltravers said:

'You are quite right. I *am* one of the people to whom things happen. Things happen to me all the time. This evening, for example, I left my wife.'

'You left her?'

Maltravers nodded. Blore-Smith did not know what to say. He could not make up his mind whether a serious matter was being treated by Maltravers with heroic restraint or, on the contrary, with almost inconceivable frivolity. Maltravers said:

'She is young and lovely and as good as she is beautiful.

33

In fact she's better. But all the same I am going to leave her.'

'Why?'

'Because,' Maltravers said, 'it is right that I should.'

He leant forward suddenly with his elbows on his knees and his chin in his hands. After a time he sighed deeply. Blore-Smith wondered whether it was his duty to say something. Thinking it better to change the subject he said:

'Didn't I see you watching the men with chains this afternoon?'

'You may have done. How like all of us.'

'Did you think so too?'

'Psychologically speaking.'

Maltravers leant forward so that his face almost touched Blore-Smith's. He said with intensity:

'Do you think that what you really need is to be put right psychologically?'

'Psycho-analysed, do you mean?'

'Something of the sort.'

Blore-Smith faltered. He had read of such things. Somehow he had never associated himself with a need for them.

'I don't know,' he said. 'Perhaps.'

Suddenly Maltravers jumped up.

'But you want life, women, a good time,' he said. 'It's no use our staying here. This isn't the sort of place where one can find any of those. Come along with me and I'll introduce you to the most beautiful woman that you have ever seen.'

By this time Blore-Smith had made up his mind that there was no escape. He was not even sure that he wanted to escape. Perhaps this was indeed what he had been looking for. He was surprised to find that, now that adventure had come his way, he was not at all certain that he was

34

going to enjoy it. He put down his glass. Maltravers hurried him into the car again and a few minutes later they stopped in front of a flower-shop.

A coloured sign hung outside inscribed, with disregard for capital letters, *la cattleya*. Underneath these words was a conventionally unconventional representation of the flower, executed by the same painter whose work Blore-Smith had seen at the Frott Gallery. Maltravers pushed at the door, which rang a bell when opened, and they went into the front of the shop. No one was there and Blore-Smith followed Maltravers towards a curtain which shut off the farther end of the room. From the other side of the curtain came Mrs. Mendoza's voice. She was saying:

'After all, why shouldn't I live in Basra if he does get a job there? It probably won't be worse than anywhere else. I shouldn't have everybody nagging at me there, living on my vitality, telling me all about themselves and their beastly affairs, and bothering me, and never giving me a moment's peace. Nor should I have to look after this wretched shop. It might be rather nice. I should be able to ride.'

Maltravers and Blore-Smith went beyond the curtain. Mrs. Mendoza and Chipchase were sitting in front of a gas fire. Chipchase, who had talked about himself all the way from the Frott Gallery, was now listening gloomily to Mrs. Mendoza's troubles. He said:

'A camel? Or a dromedary?'

'Hullo, Mendie,' Maltravers said. 'I've brought someone to see you.'

Mrs. Mendoza turned round.

'Why, Peter,' she said, 'how are you, darling? I heard the bell and thought it must be a customer.'

She stared at Blore-Smith, who wondered if he had ever felt so embarrassed. Maltravers said:

35

'This is Mr. Blore-Smith. I've just run over him in my car. To make up for doing this I thought I would bring him along to see you, Mendie.'

'But how nice.'

Mendie took Blore-Smith's hand and gave it a good squeeze while she looked at him. Blore-Smith decided that Maltravers was right. She was certainly the most beautiful woman he had ever seen. He did not know at all what sort of a person she was. Her clothes were simple and she was hardly made-up and yet at the same time there was something about her that was very arrogant, an air that he imagined rich spoilt women would have. He noticed that she had taken off her stockings and sat with her feet in a man's pair of woolly bedroom slippers. He knew that he had gone red in the face. He said:

'I hope you don't mind my coming in like this?'

'This is Mr. Chipchase,' Mendie said. 'Have a cigarette?'

Chipchase offered a limp handshake. Blore-Smith said that he did not smoke. Mrs. Mendoza took a cigarette herself. Chipchase said:

'I've just been admiring your taste in pictures.'

'My taste in pictures?'

'I was in the Frott Gallery just now.'

'Oh, yes,' said Blore-Smith. 'I think I remember seeing you there. I'm so glad you like the picture.'

'It seemed to me just a little expensive. Just a little. Of course the Frott Gallery's prices are sometimes a trifle high, there's no doubt. But they always have the best stuff.'

'I thought it a bit expensive myself,' Blore-Smith said, 'but I didn't want to miss it altogether.'

He hoped that he was giving an impression that buying pictures meant nothing to him.

'Oh, you were quite right,' Chipchase said. 'Quite right.'

36

Maltravers dragged a small settee closer to the fire and they sat down.

'How is Sarah?' Mrs. Maltravers said.

'I've left her,' Maltravers said. 'My married life is over.'

'I on the other hand am contemplating matrimony.'

'The Commodore?'

Mrs. Mendoza nodded and laughed. No one had made any effort to light her cigarette and it had remained all this time in her mouth while she moved it up and down. Blore-Smith watched this for some minutes. At last he plucked up sufficient courage to rise and take the box of matches that lay on the table beside her elbow and strike one. Mrs. Mendoza smiled beautifully at him and he began to blush again. Maltravers said:

'It would make a change if you married, Mendie.'

'I can't see that it would at all,' Chipchase said.

'I think it would be a change for the better,' Maltravers said.

Mrs. Mendoza said: 'You're both of you in a ghastly mood tonight. What on earth is wrong?'

Turning to Blore-Smith she said:

'I think he must have run over you on purpose.'

'Oh, no, I'm sure he didn't,' Blore-Smith said, and hoping to turn the conversation to something less personal added: 'Is that a Picasso hanging up there?'

Chipchase laughed harshly.

'Shut up,' Mrs. Mendoza said to him, and to Blore-Smith: 'No. It was painted by a friend of mine. I think it's rather good, don't you? I know some people don't think so. But if you're interested in pictures you must come and see the ones upstairs. I haven't space to hang them all down here.'

'I should like to very much.'

'Come along, then. Some of them are in Scrubb's room. He's my lodger. He may be working now and so will be rather bad-tempered when we disturb him but don't take any notice of what he says.

'Oh, but if it isn't convenient——'

'This way,' Mrs. Mendoza said. 'Mind the step.'

Maltravers and Chipchase were left alone. When the others could be heard moving about upstairs, Chipchase said:

'What is this you've got hold of?'

'I've no idea. I thought I'd bring it along.'

'Do you know that it's boundlessly rich?'

'How did *you* discover that?'

'It came into the Frott Gallery and paid a couple of hundred for the least inspiring picture you ever saw in your life.'

'All I know about the young gentleman is that he's bored with life and wants amusement. Women and so on. That's why I brought him here.'

'To get off with Mendie?'

'Odder things have happened.'

'You're preposterous.'

'Also I thought you might take him in hand as your first patient.'

'That, on the other hand, is a brilliant suggestion.'

'Isn't it?'

'Why shouldn't he put up the money for your film too? He's probably rich enough for that.'

Maltravers, who had been lying, apparently in a state of nervous collapse, on the sofa, sat up all at once and reached out for the cigarettes.

'That's also a very good idea,' he said. 'A very good one. How altruistic one is.'

'Will you tackle him first?'

'It's worth trying. Meanwhile you must be less morose.'

'It's important that he should respect me, to get the best results.'

The bell in the shop rang again and they heard someone come through the door. Maltravers, who always seized any opportunity of serving customers if Mrs. Mendoza was not there, got up to see who had come in. Before he had reached the shop a man put his head through the curtains and said:

'Evening, everybody.'

'Hullo,' said Maltravers and Chipchase together.

The man was about fifty. He was heavily built, with a purple weather-beaten face, and was dressed in a blue mackintosh and a bowler hat. He carried a thick malacca walking-stick.

'Mendie in?' he said.

'She's upstairs,' said Maltravers, 'showing someone the pictures. I expect she'll be down in a second.'

'Anyone I know?' said the big man, taking off his hat and mackintosh and propping up the stick against a small bookcase.

He sat down heavily and looked around the room with some suspicion. He did not seem to be altogether comfortable. Chipchase said:

'No. None of us knows him.'

'Is he a new friend of Mendie's?'

'I ran over him a short time ago,' Maltravers said. 'That is how we got to know him. I brought him along as a compensation.'

'Oh,' said the big man. 'Yes. I see.'

Cautiously he took out a pipe and began to fill it.

There was silence. Maltravers got up and, going to the foot of the staircase, shouted:

'Mendie!'

From upstairs Mrs. Mendoza yodelled.

'Someone to see you!' Maltravers shouted.

Again Mrs. Mendoza yodelled.

'Tell her not to hurry,' said the big man uneasily, and began to light his pipe.

Once more there was a long silence.

'What do you think about the slump?' said Maltravers.

The big man struck several matches and threw them away one after another, pulling away at his pipe all the time and shaking his head, by now enveloped in smoke. Before he had time to make a pronouncement Mrs. Mendoza came into the room again, followed by Blore-Smith. She said:

'Hullo, Hugo.'

The big man stood up.

'How are you?' he said and held out a wide red hand. Mrs. Mendoza took it and at the same time gave him a small kiss low on his face.

'I'm grand,' she said. 'Do you know Mr. Blore-Smith, Hugo? This is Commander Venables.'

Commander Venables shook hands with Blore-Smith, but before he sat down he went across the room to where he had hung his mackintosh on a peg and felt in one of the pockets. He found a small parcel and held it out to Mrs. Mendoza.

'This is for you,' he said.

'Hugo, the cigarette-case?'

'Yes.'

Mrs. Mendoza tore off the paper. She was excited. There was a chamois leather envelope inside. She opened it. Inside the envelope was a cigarette-case.

'Oh, Hugo, it's not the one!'

Commander Venables looked startled.

'Not the one?' he said.

'Of course it isn't!'

'But you said the modern-looking one?'

'Well, this doesn't look modern, does it?'

40

Commander Venables took the cigarette-case in his hand and examined it. He clearly found it altogether impossible to decide whether or not it looked modern.

'Oh, put it away,' Mrs. Mendoza said. 'It doesn't matter.'

'I can easily change it,' Commander Venables said.

'No. It doesn't matter in the slightest. This is a very nice one. It looks as if King Edward might have designed it for Queen Alexandra.'

'But I want you to have the one you like.'

'Don't let's say any more about it.'

'No, but look here, I say——'

'No more, Hugo, for goodness' sake.'

Mrs. Mendoza was displeased and the face of Commander Venables showed that he was only too well aware of the depths of stupidity and ignorance of which he had shown himself capable. Blore-Smith felt that as neither Maltravers nor Chipchase showed any signs of finding the situation at all awkward it was perhaps no business of his to try and ease the tension of which he himself was so conscious, but as no one spoke for some minutes he could not prevent himself from saying at last:

'I thought the pictures upstairs very interesting.'

'They are,' Maltravers said. 'I was looking at them the other day. I think they show a very strange side of Mendie's character. You know, Mendie, I think you ought to be psycho-analysed.'

'I agree with you,' Chipchase said. 'I was thinking the same myself only the other day.'

'I suppose you are going to suggest that you should do it?' Mrs. Mendoza said.

Chipchase said: 'Well, why not?'

'When I get psycho-analysed,' Mrs. Mendoza said, 'I shan't become a client of yours.'

'Very well. There is no need to be so bitter. I shall

remain friends with you even if you do happen to prefer another practitioner.'

'Have you been psycho-analysed, Captain Venables?' Maltravers said.

Commander Venables showed genuine amusement for the first time since he had come into the room. He gave several deep muffled snorts. His body shook all over and his face contracted so that it looked like a huge shrivelled fruit. Mrs. Mendoza looked at him sternly. She said:

'If you are laughing at psycho-analysis it might be as well to find out about it first.'

'I wasn't laughing at it. I was laughing because he was asking me whether I had ever had it done to me.'

'It might do you a great deal of good,' Mrs. Mendoza said. 'In fact I believe it is just what you need.'

'I think it would do you good, too,' Maltravers said. 'That is, if you don't mind my saying so. It would make you enjoy life tremendously.'

'Don't talk nonsense,' said Mrs. Mendoza, speaking as in defence of her own property threatened with outside interference. 'If Hugo decides that he wants to be psycho-analysed he can talk it over with me. I know all about it. Far more than you.'

She was in a thoroughly bad temper by this time. Suddenly she turned on Blore-Smith and said:

'I'll tell you what psycho-analysis would do for you. It would cure your stutter.'

Blore-Smith wished that the ground beneath would open open and swallow him up for ever. His stutter was a subject he was particularly sensitive about and although he could tell from Mrs. Mendoza's tone that she was only letting off steam he felt horribly uncomfortable. Before he could answer, Commander Venables, who was evidently anxious to change the subject, said:

'What I really came in about was to know what time you wanted to dine.'

'Come here at a quarter past eight,' Mrs. Mendoza said.

Commander Venables looked uncertain.

'Shall I be here at a quarter to?' he said. 'Then there would be a margin of time if you weren't ready.'

'Come at a quarter past eight. How many times do you want me to repeat it?'

Commander Venables inclined his head.

'Give me the cigarette-case,' he said, 'and I'll change it.'

'All right. If you insist.'

Commander Venables took his hat and mackintosh from the hook and his stick from the bookcase.

'Then I shall see you at eight-fifteen,' he said. 'Ready?'

'Oh, goodness me, yes,' said Mrs. Mendoza.

Commander Venables turned in the direction of Maltravers, Chipchase, and Blore-Smith. He made a movement as if to bow.

'Good hunting, gentlemen,' he said, raising his stick.

He turned about and passed through the curtain out of their sight. The bell rang once again as he opened the door of the shop. Mrs. Mendoza sat down on the sofa beside Maltravers and sighed, at the same time putting her arm around his shoulder. Chipchase said:

'I suppose I ought to be going too.'

'Why?'

'I've got to change. I'm going to the ballet.'

'Ring me up soon.'

Chipchase turned to Blore-Smith and held out his hand.

'Good-bye,' he said. 'I expect we shall see more of each other soon. I hope so anyway.'

Blore-Smith was surprised at these words because on the face of it nothing seemed to him more unlikely than that he should ever set eyes again on Chipchase. But in spite of feeling this he said as heartily as possible that he hoped it would not be long before their next meeting.

'Ring me up,' Chipchase said, giving his number. 'We'll have a meal together and talk about pictures or psycho-analysis or something of the sort.'

Chipchase then kissed Mrs. Mendoza and disappeared through the gap in the curtain. Maltravers looked at his watch. He said to Blore-Smith:

'Why not have dinner with me if you have nothing better to do? We might go to a movie afterwards if you like.'

'But really it's awfully kind of you. Of course if you want me to I'd like to dine with you enormously.'

'That's what we'll do, then,' said Maltravers. 'We'll leave when Mendie decides to go upstairs to dress.'

It was approaching nine o'clock when they reached Maltravers's club. The dining-room was empty except for waiters who stood about it in formal groups of two and three like pieces of debased classical statuary. Maltravers led the way to a table in the farthest corner of the room. From here the door they had come in by was almost out of sight. Blore-Smith knew that his cuffs were distinctly dirty and tried to forget this by staring up towards the white and gold ornamentation of the ceiling. He noticed that Maltravers's check suit seemed out of place in these surroundings, but as Maltravers seemed unconscious of any incongruity he decided that it must be all right and that perhaps it would not matter after all about his cuffs.

'Who exactly is Mrs. Mendoza?' he said.

Maltravers thrust the toast across the table in his direction. He said:

'It's not very easy to define her in three words. You've seen her, so you can judge for yourself. Nothing I could say would help very much, any more than I could describe what caviare tastes like.'

'But what does she do?'

'As you have seen, she runs a flower-shop. *la cattleya*. She has had lots of jobs and been married more than once.'

'She is certainly very beautiful,' Blore-Smith said, and although he feared that it might be indiscreet he could not prevent himself from adding:

'And who is Commander Venables?'

'He's at the back of the shop. He's in love with Mendie, as you may have noticed. He was in the Navy. Now he's got some job connected with civil aviation, I believe.'

'Oh, I see.'

'She may be going to marry him.'

'But he's years older than she is.'

'Yes,' said Maltravers, 'he is. It's all very unsatisfactory. Don't let's talk about it. We may depress ourselves. Tell me, what did you think of Chipchase, the drooping man who was sitting in the arm-chair?'

'He seemed very nice.'

Blore-Smith said this out of politeness, because what slight impression he had carried away with him of Chipchase's personality had not been favourable. Supercilious was the adjective he had applied mentally to Chipchase's manner. Supercilious and bad-tempered.

'He's a clever fellow,' Maltravers said. 'You know, if you don't mind my saying so, there was something in what Mendie said about your consulting a psychologist. Do you remember that I had suggested it just before we arrived at the shop? You might do worse than get Chipchase to take you on. That is, if he would.'

'But whatever would he do to me?'

'The mind, or rather the Ego,' said Maltravers, 'needs care as much as the body. You tell me that you are dis-

45

satisfied with life. How can you hope to enjoy life if your Ego is wrong? I ask you.'

'I suppose you can't,' Blore-Smith said, confused, 'but I still don't see what he could do.'

'If I could tell you that, I should be doing it myself. But don't let what I've said worry you. It was only a suggestion of the most conversational kind.'

'But I should like you to tell me more.'

'No, no,' Maltravers said, 'I wasn't really very serious. But if the idea interests you, talk to Chipchase about it when next you see him. He will explain everything.'

'But does he charge to do this?'

'Naturally he doesn't practise out of sheer philanthropy. What a strange notion.'

'Has he many patients?'

'I believe that he could get as many as he wants and that so far he has refused to take anyone on owing to his extreme, and to my mind rather absurd, modesty,' Maltravers said. 'But I feel that I should not have introduced the subject. I see that it has disturbed you.'

'Not at all. I am most interested in it.'

'In that case you should talk to him. But now tell me about yourself. What are your chief amusements?'

'I hardly know. I read. I walk in the park. I go to the cinema.'

'You go to the cinema? Are you interested in films?'

'Certainly I am. Aren't you? I think it's'—Blore-Smith blushed as he said this—'the most living of the arts at present.'

'It's my job,' Maltravers said. 'I write scenarios and help direct them sometimes. But it's not so much as a money-making concern that I care about it. I just use that to keep me alive. The important thing, as you say, is the film as art.'

'Oh, yes,' said Blore-Smith.

This was safer ground than discussing Maltravers's friends with him.

'The difficulty is,' Maltravers said, 'to get together all the people who feel this about the cinema. To get them together and produce uncommercial films of real social, scientific, artistic, literary, dramatic, human, and philosophic interest. That is what I hope to do one of these days.'

'It has been done to some extent already, hasn't it?' said Blore-Smith, who had by this time no idea what Maltravers was talking about.

Maltravers said: 'What I intend to do has, so far as I know, never been done in a serious manner. My proposal is nothing short of this: that I should photograph people existing.'

'What?'

'I surprise you,' Maltravers said. 'I thought I should. It is a daring scheme. Only an extension, of course, of a system that has shown itself successful in innumerable other branches of human life. But it has had to wait for me to apply it.'

'Who will you apply it to?'

'I suggest beginning on a small party of intellectuals.'

'How would you approach them?'

'To some extent psycho-analytically.'

Blore-Smith started at the repetition of this word. Maltravers said:

'A small group of people. Simply watch them behave. But no, I must not allow you to think that I am being flippant. My scheme is to represent certain human relationships in slow motion, so to speak. The films would, at present at least, have no commercial value whatever. But they would be of immense use in spreading an understanding of psychology if privately shown.'

47

'When are you going to begin doing this?'

'I have already a great deal of material collected.'

'Soon, then?'

'I must admit that considerations of a financial kind make themselves felt. I must find someone to produce, or to cause to be produced, enough money to cover the expenses that these experiments would involve.'

'Would that be a large sum?'

'Comparatively, no.'

'But you don't know exactly how much?'

Blore-Smith's voice shook a little.

'Naturally it would be hard to say accurately,' Maltravers said. 'Let me see——'

He took a small gold pencil from his pocket and began to do some calculations on the back of an envelope. After some minutes he passed the envelope to Blore-Smith and said:

'It's nothing really. Unfortunately I have not got it to spare at the moment.'

'But surely such a brilliant idea stands a good chance of success? People who have got money will come forward when they hear about it?'

'Ah,' said Maltravers, 'there you are quite right. Lots of people would come forward. But they would be unsuitable people. At heart their real interest would be in making money. One would be back again in the old world of the commercial film. What I am in search of is sincerity.'

Maltravers sighed when he said this and allowed his head to fall into his hands. Blore-Smith watched this and was moved. He too sighed. He was, indeed, genuinely interested in the film as art. He said:

'But there must be someone interested in the cinema who is both rich and sincere?'

'Find him,' Maltravers said, with intensity but without

raising his head. 'Find him and bring him to me.'

'Well, but that's absurd. I told you that I hardly knew anyone at all in London. Of course I don't know of someone like that when you yourself have not been able to find them.'

'I thought you might know of someone just down from Oxford. It would not matter what age he was. In fact it would be a good thing if he were young. We should have to keep in touch with the younger generation.'

Up to then Blore-Smith had estimated Maltravers's age at twenty-eight, but now he pushed it on to thirty, or even more. He did not want to be questioned too closely about Oxford for fear that the dullness of his own life there might be revealed in full, so he said:

'I don't think there is anyone who has just come down who would do for what you want. They weren't a very exciting crowd up with me. But what a wonderful thing it would be to help direct something like that.'

'It would have to be someone of intelligence and taste, who could supply a lot of the ideas himself.'

'I'd give anything to be able to do that.'

'Ah,' said Maltravers, 'I expect so. And you would be a very suitable person too. What a pity you have not got the money. How often one feels that about oneself and one's friends.'

Maltravers emptied the decanter into Blore-Smith's glass.

'But—but——'

Blore-Smith knew that again he was getting red in the face. It had been a day of strain and excitement of a kind to which he was quite unused. Habitually he found it difficult to make decisions about which restaurant he would eat his lunch at or what book he wanted to take out of the library. And yet the last few hours seemed to have been packed with resolutions about life of the most weighty sort, all formed on the spur of the moment. He said:

'If you meant it when you said that the venture would only cost that amount, I think—I mean, I daresay—possibly, if there was no sort of complication that turned up later—well, I might be able to find the money myself.'

'You could?'

'Of course I wouldn't have mentioned such a thing if you hadn't said that you thought that I should be a suitable person.'

'I thought so as soon as I met you. But I hardly imagined that you would be able to find the financial support.'

'Well,' said Blore-Smith, rather overcome and wondering whether perhaps he had had too much to drink, 'in that case I should be prepared to say that I would certainly put up the money. Provided, that is, that I had a certain amount of control over the concern.'

He felt it safer to add this last condition and to make his importance clear from the start. Maltravers tapped with a fork on the table. He said:

'Wait a minute. We must not go too fast. Do you realise the amount of trouble and hard work that this will let you in for? You are suggesting that you should take on what is almost a sacred trust. Are you sure that you will prove yourself worthy of it?'

'Of course I can only say that I will do my best. I'm awfully keen, if that——'

'Once decided, you will not be able to turn back,' Maltravers said. 'Think it over. Do you want to spend your money in the cause of Beauty? Wouldn't you rather invest in something more gilt-edged?'

Blore-Smith made an effort to control himself. He muttered:

'Is there anything more gilt-edged?'

Maltravers banged on the table so that the group of

waiters posed near him all jumped at the same time like a perfectly trained *corps de ballet.*

'Excellent,' Maltravers said. 'Excellent.'

Blore-Smith knew that for once he had said something worth saying. For perhaps the first time in his life he had come up to scratch.

'Will I do, then?' he said.

'Yes,' said Maltravers, 'I think you will do.'

He sat in silence with his eyes staring at the table-cloth, turning his wineglass between his finger and thumb. Blore-Smith was silent too. He was thinking of Maltravers's words: 'Once decided, you will not be able to turn back.' He was finding it difficult at that moment to reason at all clearly. He made a mental reservation that he would certainly turn back if things showed signs of going in a way of which he disapproved. This had become a great adventure. Perhaps he had begun to live. He lost himself in wild speculations until at last he heard Maltravers say:

'We will go back to my flat now and I will show you some of the stuff. Then you can think about things all tomorrow and we can meet on the next day or later in the week and discuss the views that you yourself hold. What about that?'

'There is nothing I should like better.'

'Then we can really make a start. Waiter, the bill.'

'Sit down,' said Maltravers. 'Throw those papers on the floor if they are at all in your way. It's only the manuscript of a novel my wife is writing. If you will wait here for a second I will go and get the notes I have already collected and we can run through them together.'

He went out of the room and left Blore-Smith free to examine the photographs and invitations on the mantelpiece. Blore-Smith had never before seen a room at all like this one. It surprised and to some extent shocked him to find that anyone lived and worked among all these newspapers, typewriters, and gramophone records. At the same time it made him ashamed of his own sitting-room with chintz curtains and Medici prints on the walls. He knew that after seeing this place he would never again enjoy spending an evening there reading *Vision and Design*. He would be thinking all the time of this, the wider life. He decided that he would move Van Gogh's *Sunflower* into the bedroom as soon as he reached home again. He crossed to the window. The curtains remained undrawn and he looked out on to the dark square. While he watched, a long sports car drew up in front of the house and someone got out. Then the car left the square, fast and with deafening noise. A few minutes after, Blore-Smith heard the door behind him open. Expecting that it was Maltravers who had come back to the room he turned and found that a young woman in a blue leather overcoat was standing in the doorway.

'How-do-you-do?' she said.

Blore-Smith did not know what to answer. If Maltravers had not told him earlier in the evening that he had left his wife Blore-Smith would have assumed that this was Maltravers's wife, but in the circumstances no such assumption seemed possible. At the same time he felt that, should this indeed be Mrs. Maltravers, some explanation of his own presence in the room was called for, so he said:

'Mr. Maltravers will be back in a minute. He has gone to get some papers.'

'Oh, has he?' said the young woman. 'Do sit down. I hope that he hasn't forgotten that he has left you here and gone to sleep. He sometimes does that.'

Before Blore-Smith had time to consider this possibility Maltravers came into the room again.

'Hullo,' he said to the young woman. 'You're back early.'

'Yes.'

'This is Mr. Blore-Smith, Sarah,' Maltravers said. 'You haven't met my wife yet, have you?'

Although Blore-Smith had been much impressed by Mrs. Mendoza's beauty, which was far in advance of that of any woman to whom he had previously been introduced, Sarah's appearance had an almost stronger effect on him. She was small and had her hair cut short, and the collar of her coat was turned up. There was something about her that attracted him in a disturbing way. Later he decided that it was her manner that he found so irresistible. Maltravers said:

'And how was Nipper?' and turning to Blore-Smith added: 'My wife has been dining with a racing motorist. Isn't that romantic?'

'He had a slight headache,' Sarah said, 'so he went to bed early tonight. That's why I'm back now.'

Maltravers raised his eyebrows and pursed his lips together.

'Oh?' he said. 'Oh?'

'What have you been doing?' Sarah said. She offered her cigarette-case to Blore-Smith.

'Mr. Blore-Smith has come here to discuss some business matters,' Maltravers said politely. 'Is there anything you want?'

'No,' said Sarah, 'there isn't. Except this.'

She took up one of the typewriters and held it under her arm. Blore-Smith, thinking of the smile that Mrs. Mendoza had given him for a similar act, struck a match and lit her cigarette.

'Thanks,' said Sarah. 'Good-night.'

She shut the door and a few minutes later they heard the tap-tap of typing coming from the next room.

'She's writing a novel,' Maltravers said. 'I'm the hero.'

Blore-Smith could think of no suitable reply to this piece of information, so he said nothing. He had begun to feel exhausted. Maltravers's energy seemed to increase rather than to diminish as time went on, and clearing a space on one of the tables he set out some typewritten sheets of notes and began to explain them to Blore-Smith, who did his best to listen but without much success.

'Of course this is very provisional,' Maltravers said. 'It will all have to be done in much greater detail before anything like a start can be made. At the same time it gives some idea of the scheme.'

He handed the sheets of paper one after another to Blore-Smith, sometimes making pencil notes on them as he did so.

'The pattern scenario is temporarily called *Œdipus Rex*.'

'I see.'

'It merely describes, as you see, a situation that might be photographed in certain stages of development.'

'But how would you get the people together?'

'My present scheme is that, once a good situation between a group of suitable people has been discovered, we collect them together in the same house and await developments, shooting when we think best. It's their actions that count. With the best will in the world one can't photograph a passive man subconsciously hating his father.'

'Shall we have to take a house specially for this?'

'I think that can be arranged satisfactorily. A friend of mine has a house that would be very suitable.'

'Has he agreed to lend it?'

'Not yet. But he will.'

It was after midnight by the time Maltravers had come to the end of all he had to explain. Blore-Smith was so sleepy that he wondered if he would ever have the strength to get home. The noise of Sarah's typing had stopped. Maltravers threw his pencil down on the table.

'There we are,' he said. 'That makes a beginning.'

He stood up and stretched his arms above his head.

'Are you hungry?' he said. 'I am. We'll get Sarah to cook some bacon and eggs.'

'Oh, but——'

'Sarah,' Maltravers shouted. 'Sarah!'

He went to the corner of the room and reached down behind some boxes, from the back of which he pulled out two bottles of beer. While he was opening these Sarah came into the room. She was wearing a Chinese dressing-gown over pink pyjamas.

'What do you want?' she said, rubbing her eyes. 'I was just going to sleep.'

'Will you cook us some bacon and eggs?'

'Now?'

'Of course.'

'All right. I might cook some for myself too.'

'Well, don't be long. We're famished.'

'What a life.'

'Please don't trouble as far as I'm concerned,' said Blore-Smith. 'I really don't think I want anything at all to eat. I ought to be going back, at once. Shall I be able to get a taxi outside?'

'You can't go yet,' Maltravers said. 'You must stay and have something. We can call you up taxi at any time.'

'No, don't go,' Sarah said. 'The eggs will be ready in a second. I've begun to feel quite hungry myself.'

'Can't I help you?' said Blore-Smith, although he had only a vague idea of how to cook bacon and eggs.

'Oh, don't bother to be polite,' said Maltravers, who had gone back to the papers on the table, but he took no active steps to prevent Blore-Smith from following Sarah into the kitchen.

'Look,' she said. 'Do you mind giving these plates a bit of a polish up with this cloth?'

For some minutes he stood watching the eggs being cooked and handing her objects she asked for.

'There,' said Sarah, 'will you take yours? I'll bring these along on the tray.'

They returned to the sitting-room, where Sarah laid the table. Maltravers poured out some beer.

'How is your book getting on?' he said to Sarah.

'It's finished.'

'Why haven't you shown it to me?'

'I only finished it this morning.'

"Well, I've seen you since then, haven't I?'

'You didn't show much sign of wanting to hear about it when you came in this afternoon.'

'You never mentioned it.'

'I didn't think it would interest you.'

'I take a great interest in your work,' Maltravers said. 'More than you do in mine, I'm afraid.'

Blore-Smith noticed that Maltravers, perhaps experiencing a reaction from the energetic mood he had been in all the evening, now seemed to be working himself up into a rage. Feeling nervous as to the consequences of this, should it be the case, Blore-Smith said to Sarah:

'What sort of book are you writing?'

'A novel,' Maltravers said. 'I told you. I'm the hero.'

'You're not,' Sarah said. 'You're not in it now at all. I had to take you out. You were such a boring character.'

'What?'

'You are just mentioned right at the end as a half-mad tramp who comes into a public-house and frightens some commercial travellers.'

'So that's what you think of me, is it?'

'That's all you are in the book.'

'Of course I've known for ages that that is how you regard me,' Maltravers said, putting a lot of pepper over his egg.

The three of them ate in silence for some minutes after he had said this. At last Blore-Smith, again speaking to Sarah, said:

'We've been talking about the film.'

'What film?' Sarah said.

'*Œdipus Rex.*'

'I haven't seen it. Where is it on?'

'The private uncommercial film your husband thinks of organising.'

Blore-Smith was surprised that he had to explain this. Maltravers said:

'You haven't heard about it yet. I shall tell you in due time.'

'Are you blossoming out into a film director?'

'Ask no questions. I shall inform you when I think fit.'

'How frightfully exciting.'

'Meanwhile you must try and learn to cook bacon better.'

'What is wrong with this?'

'It doesn't taste like bacon.'

Sarah turned to Blore-Smith.

'What do you think?' she said.

Blore-Smith stuttered:

'I? Well, it seems to me very good on the whole. Perhaps a little salt. Excellent really.'

After he had said this Blore-Smith looked with apprehension at Maltravers, who showed no mark of having heard what he had said. Sarah smiled at Blore-Smith, who at once felt glad that he had taken her side and even regretted that he had not said more in defence of her bacon. Maltravers put down his knife and fork.

'I'm going to bed now,' he said. 'I'm rather tired. I've

57

had a busy day. Will you ring me up when you have thought all these things out?'

He held out a hand to Blore-Smith, who shook it and was too surprised and tired himself to say more than good-night. Passing his hand across his forehead, Maltravers sighed and left the room. Sarah began to clear away the plates.

'Poor dear,' she said. 'He hasn't been very well lately.'

"Is he often like this?'

'Not well?'

'No—I mean—at least—yes. Is he often not well?'

'On and off.'

Sarah yawned.

'I really must be going now,' Blore-Smith said. 'I'm afraid I've been a great nuisance staying so long.'

'Nonsense. Do you want a taxi? There's the number.'

While he was waiting for the taxi to arrive Blore-Smith nerved himself to say:

'I do hope that we shall meet again.'

'Of course we shall. Especially if the film gets under way.'

'Yes,' said Blore-Smith, remembering the film. 'Of course.'

'You must ring me up and come to see me.'

'May I really do that?'

'Do you think you will be able to find something for me to do in the film? Writing dialogue or designing sets or something?'

'Oh, but I'm sure that your husband will arrange for that, won't he, if you'd like something like that?'

'I'm not so sure.'

'You see, it will all be more or less extempore, I suppose. No studio work. But do you do much work for films?'

'No. None really. I'm motoring correspondent for *Mode*.

Did I tell you that? Are you interested in cars?'

'Well, no, not much,' said Blore-Smith. 'But I suppose you are?'

'I go down on my knees to them.'

'To cars?'

'They're my religion.'

'Oh.'

'I'll take you out in my car some time,' Sarah said. 'Be sure and ring me up.'

Outside in the square the taxi hooted a few times. Blore-Smith said good-night again and groped his way to the foot of the stairs. On the way home he went to sleep, and when they arrived at Ebury Street he was roused by the taxi-man shaking his arm.

The next morning Blore-Smith found that he had a slight headache. He lay in bed thinking about the previous day, trying to recall all that had taken place. After a time he contrived to sort out in his mind some of the things that had happened to him.

Pondering over them, he became convinced that he had behaved in a silly manner. He got out of bed. While he was shaving he decided that if Maltravers tried to get into touch with him he would excuse himself on the grounds that he had had too much to drink and in this way extricate himself from the entanglement.

He sat indoors all the morning and every time the telephone bell rang he prepared himself for making a speech to this effect. But all the telephone calls turned out to be wrong numbers, and by the end of the day Blore-Smith found himself in a highly nervous state. As usual he had dinner alone. Not in his rooms, to which he found that he had taken a sudden dislike, but at a small restaurant in the neighbourhood controlled by distressed gentlewomen.

Contrary to his usual custom, he sent out for half a bottle of St. Emilion, but this did not cheer him up so much as he had hoped. After dinner he went to a cinema, but the film was so poor that he came out half-way through and walked about the streets for some time to avoid arriving home before it was time to go to bed.

The next day passed in much the same way. He heard nothing from Maltravers. By this time Blore-Smith had tried to reconsider the situation and had begun to think that perhaps his first conclusions about the scheme had been justifiable after all. Since meeting Maltravers time seemed to hang on his hands more heavily than ever before.

On the second evening he stayed in his room and read, but he found that he was unable to concentrate on either law books or novels. That night he slept badly.

He woke up on the third day convinced that he was behaving like a fool. Maltravers had given him the chance of a lifetime and he had taken no steps to follow up a suggestion which he realised now had been presented to him in so unblatant a form that many of its best points had at first escaped him. He made up his mind that if he heard nothing of Maltravers during that day he would write to him in the evening and ask when it would be convenient for them to have another discussion about the matter in hand. He would have telephoned if he had not felt too embarrassed to use this form of communication. Again the day passed so slowly that he thought the evening would never come. Apart from anything else he wanted to see Sarah Maltravers again. After tea Blore-Smith sat down and began to compose a letter.

While he was doing this the telephone bell rang. Blore-Smith lifted the receiver. It was Chipchase, asking if he might pay a call.

Blore-Smith's first sensation on discovering the name of

the speaker was a renewal of his earlier suspicions, but as Chipchase did not mention Maltravers and because Blore-Smith was only too anxious to have someone to talk to at any price he said:

'Yes, yes. Of course I remember meeting you. Do come round. I was meaning to ring you up but I mislaid your number.'

'All right,' Chipchase said, speaking very indistinctly. 'I'll be round quite soon.'

Blore-Smith sat down and tried to size up his hopes and fears. He wondered whether or not he should take Chipchase into his confidence. Chipchase was the only person he knew who could possibly tell him anything about Maltravers. At the same time Chipchase was Maltravers's friend and would therefore be biased in his favour. When the front-door bell rang Blore-Smith was still unable to make up his mind. He felt thoroughly uneasy. Chipchase's manner did not reassure him.

'Won't you put your hat and coat there?'

Chipchase did so and sat down in silence. Blore-Smith was uncomfortable. He had the impression that Chipchase's bearing was intended to convey in suitable terms the arrival of a gloomy genius in this humble place. He remembered suddenly that there was nothing to drink in the house. He said:

'I'm afraid I haven't got anything to offer you to drink. I'm so sorry.'

'I don't want a drink, thanks very much,' Chipchase said. 'I have indigestion, as a matter of fact.'

'Oh? I'm so sorry.'

'It doesn't matter,' Chipchase said. 'I shall get over it. It's a form of compulsion-neurosis due, I think, to jealousy. I suppose the Frott Gallery haven't sent your picture along yet?'

61

'Oh, no. I can't expect it for a long time yet. The show has only just begun,' Blore-Smith said, wondering whether he should ask Chipchase straight away what he thought of Maltravers's proposal.

This problem was solved by Chipchase himself, who said:

'Did you have an amusing dinner the other night after you left Mendie?'

'Very enjoyable. How nice Mr. Maltravers is. Afterwards I went back to his flat. In fact I had bacon and eggs there at the end of the evening.'

'Did you meet Sarah?'

'She cooked the eggs.'

'Didn't you like her?'

'She's charming,' Blore-Smith said. 'Awfully nice.'

'I think they are such a good couple,' Chipchase said. 'Made for each other.'

This view of the Maltravers household had not immediately recommended itself to Blore-Smith, who was so surprised at what Chipchase had said that he looked closely at his face to see if he might perhaps be joking. As Chipchase's features had all the appearance of seriousness, Blore-Smith replied with some remark about Sarah's attractive way of dressing. Chipchase agreed.

'They are lucky to have found each other,' he said.

'Have they been married long?'

'About two years. There was a lot of opposition on the part of Sarah's family. Then her old father died suddenly. I think she must have poisoned him.'

'What?'

'Well, perhaps not. Anyway the old man must have had his suspicions, because he left most of his money to found a home for fallen women or something of the sort. That was because he disapproved of Maltravers.'

'Why did he disapprove?'

'Well,' said Chipchase, 'you've seen him, haven't you?'

'Maltravers?'

'Yes.'

'But was it just his clothes?'

'That sort of thing and the way he talked and the things he did. Maltravers gave up the civil service and got a job in pictures, which Sarah's father considered to be falling as low as it is possible to fall.'

'Did he sell pictures or paint them?'

'Not that sort of picture. Films. He went into the movie business.'

'Oh, of course. I knew he was doing that.'

'His own family wanted him to become a colonial governor or a permanent under-secretary or something of the sort, but I expect that in their hearts they realised that in the long run he would do much more harm to more people in a job like that than he would ever be able to do in the cinema trade.'

'But why should he do harm?'

'I don't mean harm in the bad sense, you know.'

Blore-Smith wondered what other harm there was, but he did not like to ask repeatedly for explanations of everything that Chipchase said to him and so he did not reply. His interest in these facts about Maltravers's private life had made him forget about the projected scheme for uncommercial films. Chipchase continued to talk. He talked about Maltravers, about Sarah, about plays, about painting, about books, about food, and about women. Then he got up suddenly and said:

'It's been very nice meeting again. I must go now. Will you ring me up some time?'

He had taken up his hat and coat and nearly reached the door before Blore-Smith could collect himself sufficiently to mention the subject that was now uppermost in his mind.

'There was something that Maltravers said to me the other night——' Blore-Smith began, and then he stopped, not knowing how best to word what he wanted to ask.

'Yes?'

'He said he wanted to make an uncommercial film. He said he wanted someone to put up some money——'

'Well?'

'He suggested that I should do this, as I think I could probably raise the amount he mentioned.'

'I congratulate you,' Chipchase said. 'You must have made a very good impression on him. It sounds a magnificent idea.'

Blore-Smith was taken by surprise. He said:

'Yes. I think so.'

'I shall enormously look forward to seeing the film when it is shown,' Chipchase said.

Again he prepared to leave the room. Blore-Smith in some agitation said:

'I wanted to ask you—do you think—you see, I don't know Mr. Maltravers at all——'

'No, of course you don't. You only met him the other day when you came to Mendie's, didn't you?'

'Shall I do it?'

'But it's the chance of a lifetime.'

'You think so?'

'I'm sure of it.'

'I—I suddenly became suspicious.'

'Why?'

'I don't know. I sometimes get like that. I think I'm rather nervy.'

Chipchase began to take off his overcoat.

'Look here,' he said, 'I'll stay a bit longer. You tell me all about yourself.'

64

'How do you mean?'

'Your nerves.'

'What shall I tell you?'

'Everything.'

'Where shall I begin?'

'Describe your symptoms.'

'I can't make up my mind to do anything. I'm bored. I can't sleep. I'm frightened of people.'

'In fact you have a strong feeling of inferiority? Yes?'

'At times.'

'The uncertainty that you feel about Maltravers and this film is typical?'

'Absolutely.'

Blore-Smith did not think it necessary to add that such problems as these did not arise in his life every day.

'People seem to be persecuting you all the time?'

'Sometimes.'

'You give way to day-dreams?'

'At intervals.'

'How often?'

'I don't know. Once or twice a day perhaps. I don't remember exactly.'

'Do you mean that you don't want to remember?'

'Yes—I mean no.'

'You are ambitious?'

'No, not at all.'

'Of course you are!'

'I suppose in some ways.'

'Do you ever have delusions of grandeur?'

'No.'

Blore-Smith was emphatic this time.

'You are sure?'

'Quite sure.'

'Do you,' said Chipchase, coming closer, 'ever feel an over-powering impulse to cruelty?'

'Good heavens, no.'

'A slight one, then?'

'No, I don't think so.'

'Come, come,' said Chipchase. 'Admit you feel a slight one.'

'Perhaps,' said Blore-Smith, wretchedly.

There was a pause. Chipchase put his hands in his pockets and walked towards the window. Without turning round he said:

'Have you ever thought of taking any sort of psycho-analytical or similar treatment?'

'Well, Maltravers suggested something of the sort—and —and Mrs. Mendoza,' said Blore-Smith, remembering the reference to his stutter.

'It would be worth considering.'

'You think so?'

'Especially if you are going to embark on the film-directing business. You will need to have strong nerves to stand the strain of the people you will meet in the movie world. Make up your mind to that.'

'Are you—do you do it yourself?'

'Do what?'

'Give treatment?'

'That is how I propose to demonstrate some of my own developments of the science.'

'And do you think it would make me feel better?'

'Of course no definite promise can be made. There is every reason to suppose that, given time and application on your part, your own state might be improved.'

'Would you take me as a patient?'

'Why?' said Chipchase. 'This is very unexpected.'

'I should be so pleased if——'

66

'I should have to think about it. Are you sure that you really want me to?'

'I think it would be a great help to me if you would.'

'It would cost you a certain amount of money, you know.'

'Naturally. But are the fees high?'

Chipchase took a card from his pocket and held it towards Blore-Smith, who took it and read the figures written on it.

'I see,' he said, 'I see.'

He thought for a few moments, remembering that he had other commitments on his hands. There was a pause. Chipchase lit a cigarette. At last Blore-Smith said:

'I think I could manage that.'

'It is very important,' Chipchase said, 'that treatment should continue uninterrupted for a reasonably long time. It would not do, for example, if you suddenly went away for a month in the middle.'

'No, I see that. But what should I do if I had to? In connection with the film, for instance?'

'The only thing would be for the treatment to be continued wherever you went.'

'By some local practitioner?'

'No, no. It is vitally important that there should be no change of that kind.'

'Perhaps you would be able to accompany me?'

'That would be the only satisfactory way.'

'Would you be able to do this?'

'It might be arranged.'

'There is, of course, no prospect of my going away at present.'

'Excellent. But one never knows. When would you wish to start the treatment?'

'Would the next week or so be too soon?'

67

'I think I could manage that,' Chipchase said.

He wrote down his address on the back of his tariff card. 'Come here at eleven o'clock on Monday week,' he said, 'and we will have our first session. I shall look forward to seeing you.'

He took his hat and coat from the chair.

'Good-bye,' he said.

'Good-bye,' said Blore-Smith, opening the door.

When he heard the front door shut, Blore-Smith crossed to the window and, drawing the lace curtains aside, he watched Chipchase sidling up the street. Once more his head was in a whirl. He wondered what had come over him during the last few days. He sat down in the arm-chair and clasped together his hands.

It was some time before Maltravers and Chipchase had the opportunity to meet again and discuss matters. This was because Maltravers had been offered a temporary job at some film studios which, although inconsiderable financially, was important from the point of view of keeping in touch and occupied most of his day. Chipchase had been busy with odds and ends of journalism. Both of them kept up with Blore-Smith, Maltravers by telephone and Chipchase at his own flat, where he held one or two preliminary examinations of his new patient's conscious and subconscious mind. On the whole the necessary arrangements by which they were to take over the reorganisation of Blore-Smith's life seemed to be going forward in a manner satisfactory to all parties concerned. A hint of spring was in the air now, so that when at last Maltravers and Chipchase contrived to meet it was decided that dinner at a road-house would supply a suitable environment for talking over ways and means.

As they drove down a by-pass road between bright-

coloured filling-stations and neo-Tudor cafés, Chipchase
said:

'Well? What are we going to do with this male Madame
Bovary now we have got him?'

In the distance before them, growing obscure in the light
of evening, there were trees behind the brick and tin houses
that lined the macadam. Maltravers accelerated, jumping
the amber light of the traffic signals. He said:

'It is now arranged that I go to Berlin next month.'

'And I shall be left here holding the baby.'

'I can't risk throwing up the Berlin job. You will have
to keep him in play till it's over. It will only last a month
or two.'

'It had occurred to me that I might take him to Paris for
a few weeks. Half the trouble is that he has never been
anywhere. He could shake off a few inhibitions there and
then we could join you in Berlin for a little research work
in the art of the cinema.'

'What a very good idea. By the way, Caroline is in Paris
now, isn't she?'

'Is she? Perhaps we shall meet. One will be very busy,
of course.'

'How serious a case do you think he is?'

'I shall earn every penny of my emoluments. I can assure
you of that. No human being ever needed treatment more.'

'It always makes life pleasanter,' Maltravers said, 'to feel
that one is living honestly. It is just the same about his
attitude to the cinema. I know that I am combining business with genuine philanthropy. So often one has to get
money in such sordid ways.'

'True.'

'As a matter of fact,' Maltravers said, 'I always look upon
myself as a gentleman, however badly I behave. I'm like
those women who after having dozens of lovers still

secretly regard themselves as pure. Everything is done with a sort of mental reservation like having one's fingers crossed.'

Chipchase said: 'I don't feel like that any longer. I've sunk. I can therefore take far more credit for the few gentlemanly actions I do than persons like yourself who ought really to be doing them all the time.'

'Perhaps that is a wiser attitude. I suppose you will come to Berlin, too?'

'Naturally.'

'By the way, in the course of your preliminary talks with him has he said anything about Sarah?'

'There is a woman who sounds uncommonly like her who is evidently obsessing him.

'It is undoubtedly Sarah. I had a strong suspicion that he was going to fall for her.'

'Is she furious?'

'I don't think she knows anything about it yet.'

'Would she be coming with you to Germany?'

'I don't know. She may have engagements in London.'

'Nipper?'

'I take it.'

The road bifurcated and they turned left and roared up a hill and out into the country. Soon they were passing between hedges and fields. Chipchase said:

'Then I will go ahead with arrangements for visiting Paris without further reference for the moment to your plans.'

'Act quite independently. Paris should be very enjoyable at this time of year. The trees will be coming out.'

'We will start at the beginning of next week. I will keep you informed as to developments. '

'I shall look forward to Berlin too. You know, I haven't had a real holiday since I've been married.'

'No?'

'I may let myself go,' Maltravers said.

He parked the car at the end of a row of other cars and took a numbered ticket from the hand of an attendant dressed in a green leather jerkin, a hood, and buckled shoes. They went up the steps and under a portcullis. A girl in a steeple hat and wimple took their coats. Sounds of music were coming from the room inside.

# 2

BLORE-SMITH sat in his room, attending respectfully to Chipchase, who stood in front of the mantelpiece, outlining their plan of campaign. Van Gogh's *Sunflower* and the miniature reproduction of the Colleone statue had been taken away, and Blore-Smith had fixed his eyes on a spot beyond Chipchase's head where the picture from the Frott Gallery, unexpectedly prompt in arriving, now hung. Some bottles were ranged along the sideboard. Blore-Smith had just ended his account of the nightmare he had experienced on Tuesday and he lay back relaxed and exhausted on the sofa. Chipchase shut his notebook and put his fountain pen into his pocket. He said:

'And so I shall leave all the arrangements in connection with our visit to Paris in your hands. It will bring you into touch with life and will encourage you to leave behind the dream world in which you have become accustomed to live.'

Blore-Smith gave a start and blushed.

'What exactly shall I have to do?' he said.

'Tickets. Passports. Money changing. I will show you my passport, which will tell you where to apply.'

'How are we going?'

'I think it will be best to fly. It is quickest. And on the whole the most comfortable.'

'Will you look through the things after I have got them?'

'I will check everything.'

Some days later, after running through the stuff, Chipchase was glad to find that all the items were in order.

It was sunny weather when they arrived at Croydon.
Blore-Smith stood and listened to the fretful noise of the
machines as they left the green lawns of the airport. He
watched them uneasily as they swept up and disappeared
at last in clouds. He had never before been in an aeroplane.

'Come on,' said Chipchase. 'Up the steps.'

Blore-Smith obeyed. Soon he was watching England
splayed out enigmatically below him. Chipchase, reading
*The Occult Review,* which he had bought at the airport
bookstall, sat moodily beside him. For some time neither
of them spoke, and then Blore-Smith said:

'Look. The sea.'

'Yes.'

'What are those mauve patches on the water? Are they
seaweed? Is it so clear that we can see the bottom?'

'Cloud-shadows.'

'Don't they look strange on the blue water?'

'Like bruises on a body.'

Blore-Smith did not answer. He continued to look
through the glass at the waves, which became more grey
as they flew on. Chipchase said:

'We're running into bad weather.'

The plane began to rock about, sinking violently into air-
pockets that seemed bottomless, racing through banks of
dark cloud. Blore-Smith found himself tiring of the vibra-
tion and for a time he clutched a paper bag, wondering
whether he would be able to hold out until they reached
their destination. Chipchase had folded up *The Occult
Review* and sat staring in front of him. His face looked
like grey marble. He, too, toyed with a bag for some
minutes, but after a time he folded it up and returned it to
its pocket on the wall. Several other passengers were less

73

fortunate. At last they arrived at Le Bourget.

'Whereabouts are we going to stay?' Blore-Smith said, as they climbed into the bus.

Chipchase said: 'On what George Augusta Sala refers to as the Surrey side of the Seine. '

It was a small hotel and the hall smelt of cinnamon. After the boxes had been taken up to their rooms Chipchase grunted loudly.

'And now,' he said, 'we'll have a *fine* to settle our stomachs after all we have been through.'

'Can we go to the Latin Quarter?' said Blore-Smith.

'Yes. We will. We'll go and have a *fine* in the Latin Quarter.'

Blore-Smith followed Chipchase down the stairs of the hotel and out into the street. This was the first time he had been out of England. He looked around him with surprise, trying to remember any French that he might have learnt at school. He had never before felt himself so entirely in the hands of his psycho-analyst. A sinking despair overcame him as they left the long narrow street along which they had been walking and began to cross the Luxembourg Gardens. Everyone they had come in contact with since crossing the Channel had seemed to be in a bad temper. Life in this city of new smells and unfamiliar light was evidently lived on a different plane from anything he had been used to. He tried to cheer himself up with the thought that he was about to see Montparnasse, of which he had heard so much.

'Shall we go to an artists' café,' he said.

'Yes, we'll go to an artists' café,' said Chipchase, 'but try not to over-excite yourself. You must learn to develop a more level view of life.'

'I can't help feeling excited.'

Sometimes Blore-Smith felt almost petulant at the way

Chipchase treated him. He only bore it in silence because he realised that in the long run it was all for his own good. He said:

'I've always wanted to see Montparnasse.'

'Well, here you are, then.'

'This?'

'All of it.'

They had debouched into a broad boulevard which at first sight seemed to be fronted entirely with super-cafés. Chairs and tables stretched away into the distance as far as the eye could reach. At this time of day the *terrasses* were almost deserted except for waiters who stood, flicking napkins at insects, real or imaginary, and watching the passers-by with sallow disapproving faces.

'Which one shall we go to?' Chipchase said. 'There is very little to choose.'

'Could we go to the Dôme?'

'Very well. We will go to the Dôme.'

They sat down at a table and Chipchase ordered drinks. Blore-Smith looked around him. A curious sweetish smell that he found sickly and not altogether agreeable hung about the place. Three Americans sat at a neighbouring table, hunched up and swaying in their thick tubular clothes, while they argued with each other about a poker game of the previous night. While Blore-Smith watched them they were joined by a fourth American, who, on his arrival at the table, said to one of those already seated: 'And did you make her?' To which the other replied: 'And did I make her?' at the same time knocking over and on to the floor with his elbow a pile of saucers, some of which broke while others rolled away along the pavement.

'Who are those?' Blore-Smith said.

'Artists,' said Chipchase. 'And now I want to say a little more about how we are going to live. We shall be very quiet but at the same time have a look at everything. There are certain barriers that you have got to break down, but there is no reason, in my opinion, why you should go at them too violently.'

'No, no.'

Blore-Smith felt relieved by these words. Chipchase said:

'That is why I thought it best that you should come abroad with me first. I like doing things quietly. If you begin to feel that life with me is too slow, remember that there will be plenty of opportunity for more excitement when we meet Maltravers in Berlin in a few weeks' time. He has a great deal of energy.'

'Oh, but I like being quiet——'

'Yes'—Chipchase paused in his conversation to watch a *midinette,* carrying a cardboard hat-box with a bright flowered design all over it, pass their table—'at present that is all right. But there is danger that you may allow this taste to grow into a resistance to life. You understand what I mean?'

'Yes, but——'

'Very well then. There is no need to discuss it any more now. I thought I would just mention it to you.'

Before Blore-Smith could answer, Chipchase had begun to wave his hand to a man who was walking up the street, and at the same time to shout:

'Gaston! Gaston!'

The man, who was tall and slim and dressed in a light grey check suit, was of indeterminate nationality. He had a slight moustache and was clearly intended to look English, but there was something unconvincing about this highly perfected character-part, so that in the end he might have been a member of any cosmopolitan society, Scandinavian, Austrian, Hungarian, or American. His face was a flat dead white in colour and very smooth. When he saw Chipchase he paused, threw up his hands, and then vaulted over a café table to reach the place where they were sitting.

'*Ah, mon vieux,*' he said. 'How's life?'

'Have a drink?'

'Did I ever refuse?'

'This is Mr. Blore-Smith,' Chipchase said. 'Monsieur de la Tour d'Espagne.'

'*Enchanté,*' said the Frenchman, nodding formally, but at the same time managing to convey that he omitted to shake hands because he understood that it was an un-English habit rather than because he wished to be stand-offish. 'Are you over for long?'

'A week or ten days,' Chipchase said. 'Mr Blore-Smith is a client of mine. I thought that a little Paris air might do him good while we proceeded with the psycho-analytical treatment that he is undergoing at my hands.'

M. de la Tour d'Espagne looked surprised. He said:

'*Ah, le psychanalyse?*'

'That's it,' said Chipchase. 'And how are you, Gaston?'

'Top-hole, old man.'

He talked really excellent English, flavoured with an occasional touch of pre-war slang which lent an old-world charm to his conversation.

'You have seen Schlumbermayer?'

'No. Is he in Paris?' Chipchase said.

'But of course. He is over on business. Buying pictures and furniture.'

'How very extravagant.'

'And what pictures do you think he is buying?'

'Dirty pictures.'

'No. You are wrong. He is buying the famous La Tour d'Espagne collection.'

'No?'

'Well, he is having a look at it and he will certainly buy something out of it.'

'But why are you selling?'

M. de la Tour d'Espagne raised his hands.

'Well, you see, times are pretty rotten,' he said. 'And then I don't go there often. I am trying to let the house to some South Americans. After all, one must live.'

'I suppose so.'

'Why not meet us all to-morrow night? Pauline is giving a party *à la Vache enragée*. She would love to see you, I know. Bring your friend along. Everybody will be there, including Schlumbermayer, as a matter of fact.'

'That sounds perfect,' Chipchase said; and, turning to Blore-Smith, added: 'Pauline is the Duchesse de Borodino. You must certainly meet her. She is one of the most delightful people in the whole of France.'

'I should like to very much,' said Blore-Smith sincerely.

'Come about eleven o'clock,' said M. de la Tour d'Espagne. 'And now I must be going.'

He got up from the table, shuddered violently, and grimaced.

'I must go at once now,' he said. His face twitched a little. 'Awfully glad to have seen you. *A demain.*'

He set off up the street at a great rate.

'Why did he go so suddenly?' Blore-Smith said.

Chipchase screwed up his eyes.

'Goodness knows,' he said. 'I expect he had a date.'

'Who is he?'

'He's called the Marquis de la Tour d'Espagne. An anglicised Frenchman,' Chipchase said. 'Never an entirely satisfactory product, for some reason.'

'Why not?'

'It's a synthesis that doesn't seem to work. I don't know why. But with all his failings Gaston can be very charming.'

'Why is he so white?'

'He smokes too much,' Chipchase said, and laughed.

They spent the morning strolling the rue de Seine, look-ing at the picture galleries. Blore-Smith found that after a night's rest he was on the whole feeling better, although the change of air had affected his inside and the alien surroundings still caused him some misgivings. He found that he had to keep his wits about him in case he might be called upon to speak French. Chipchase could on occa-sions produce some unexpected regional colloquialism, but apart from this his knowledge of the language was severely limited and he insisted on Blore-Smith doing all the talking on the grounds that it was psychologically good for him to make contacts with foreigners in this way.

'The first thing you must do,' Chipchase said, as they walked in the direction of the river, 'is to develop a healthier attitude towards women. Be firm with them. They won't bite you. Not immediately, anyway.'

'Will there be a lot of women to-night?'

'What do you mean?'

'At the Duchesse's party?'

'There will be some certainly. And there will be a lot in the places where we shall go.'

'Oh.'

'Littered about.'

'Professional?' said Blore-Smith with an effort.

'Of course.'

Chipchase did not pursue this subject. Instead he said:

'We will have a nice little lunch now and after that we will go to the cinema. Then we can return to the hotel and I will take some notes on your state. After that we will find somewhere pleasant for a drink and dine well and late so that we can go straight on from dinner and join

79

the others. What do you think of that?'

'All right.'

'Here's a taxi.'

Chipchase told the man an address and got in after Blore-Smith, who sat in the corner and began to think about Sarah Maltravers. He found that lately his mind had dwelt more and more on this subject. He wondered what this could mean, and supposed that it had something to do with the changes that were undoubtedly taking place in his attitude towards life. He could not help wishing that his visit to Paris was over and that he was back in England again. He was roused from these musings by Chipchase's voice saying:

'Will you pay this fellow off, while I go and find a table?'

Blore-Smith did his best with the taxi-man. Then he went into the restaurant, where he found Chipchase, who had already begun to order lunch.

'Sit down,' said Chipchase, 'and I will tell you about some of the people we are going to meet tonight. What do you want to drink?'

'Vichy,' said Blore-Smith. 'Go on.'

'I think I might have half a bottle of something white. Well, first of all there is Pauline de Borodino. You remember Napoleon made them kings of Cyprus or some such place. She knows everyone in Europe of the slightest interest.'

'Does she talk English?'

'Better than Gaston. Now Gaston is rather another matter. He is not Napoleonic. He is medieval in the worst sense, and when he has had a few drinks he sometimes behaves like a minor character in Proust who has got out of hand. When he begins to speak of the blood of Bayard flowing in his veins, don't argue with him.'

'I shouldn't dream of arguing——'

'Very well. But remember: the blood of Bayard is a danger-signal.'

'And who is Schlumbermayer?'

'Schlumbermayer,' Chipchase said, 'I shall not attempt to describe. It will be sufficient for you to know that he is a collector, has a large and hideous house near London, and is somewhere between the ages of forty and fifty. His character repays study, so, if you get an opportunity to-night, talk to him.'

'What does he collect?'

'Everything. Pictures, furniture, carpets, pots and pans, rare editions, armour, stamps, matchboxes, tram-tickets—everything.'

'What does he do with it all?'

'He sells a certain amount and keeps the rest in cellars.'

'Who else?'

'There will probably be some Americans with foreign titles. You must not be surprised at anything this crowd say or do.'

'I'll try not to be.'

'Some of them are distinctly eccentric. And, I warn you, French fairies are the last straw.'

The afternoon passed quickly and pleasantly. By dinner-time Blore-Smith had thrown off his depression and was feeling very happy. He continually reminded Chipchase of his gratitude at having been brought to Paris.

They dined, as Chipchase had suggested, well. The panelled room was dimly lighted, and sitting back in his chair, drinking coffee, Blore-Smith felt full of suppressed excitement at the thought of the evening before him.

'What shall we have now?' Chipchase said. 'Brandy? Armagnac?'

'I should like to try something I have not tasted before.'

'Very good. Excellent. That is just how you should be feeling. How about some calvados?'

'Yes.'

Blore-Smith was feeling better than he had felt for ages. Perhaps better than he had ever felt in his life before. He turned the liqueur glass between his finger and thumb and assumed as well as he was able the sluggish prudential expression of a connoisseur.

'How do you like it?'

'Excellent.'

'Another one?'

'Yes.'

'It will be time to start soon. You'd better begin asking for the bill. I'll be back in a second.'

Blore-Smith, out of sheer lightness of heart, ordered another calvados for himself while Chipchase was out of the room and drank it quickly before he reappeared.

'Did I leave enough?' he said later when they were in the taxi.

'Quite enough,' Chipchase said. 'Far too much, in fact. Still, it doesn't matter. One's only young once.'

Blore-Smith noticed that Chipchase as well as himself seemed to be in much better form than usual. It was also clear from his manner that it was the calvados that had made him unbend. He had become rather flushed in the cheeks. Soon they arrived at the entrance of what was evidently a night-club of the most discreet kind. A small sign stuck out from above the door on which were the words: 'à la Vache enragée'.

The place surprised, and to some extent disappointed, Blore-Smith by the quietness of its black-and-gold decorations. A Cuban band, in coloured shirts and cummerbunds, was playing in muted pessimistic tones in one corner. The clients sitting at the tables round the room or up at the bar seemed on the whole equally subdued, but a certain amount of noise and laughter came from the corner of the room opposite the band where M. de la Tour d'Espagne sat with a number of other men and women. When he saw Chipchase and Blore-Smith, the Marquis jumped up and said:

'Splendid of you to come.'

After the introductions, which left him hopelessly confused, Blore-Smith found himself separated from Chipchase and sitting between the Duchesse de Borodino herself and a young negro wearing a dinner-jacket. The rest of the party, only some of whom were in evening dress, included two middle-aged American women in expensive clothes, introduced as Princess Marquetto and Mrs. Rausch, a mousy little Frenchwoman dressed in black who never spoke, a bald American, possibly Mrs. Rausch's husband, the Colonel Teape who had been in the Frott Gallery just before Blore-Smith's arrival there, Schlumbermayer, whom Blore-Smith recognised at once; and two or three others, at the far end of the table, amorphous entities whom Blore-Smith was unable to distinguish one from another. Chipchase took his place among these last.

Pauline de Borodino sat at the head of the table, a tremendous Rowlandsonesque Catherine the Great or Maria Theresa. She had a bottle of champagne in each hand and was filling all the glasses within her orbit. Whilst she did this she talked to Blore-Smith, who was thinking that never before in all his life had he seen anything like her.

'How long are you over here? It's awfully nice of you to come tonight. I expect you know Paris well. I wonder why we have never met before. Do try some of this champagne. It's a special brand that I make them keep here for me. Have you known Oliver Chipchase long? Do you want a stick to take the fizz out? What do you think of it? It's dry isn't it, in the English way? He is a very old friend of mine. Do you know Peter Maltravers too?'

'Yes, I do. He and I are going to produce an uncommercial film together.'

Blore-Smith suddenly felt that he wanted to tell her all about his life.

'A film? You are going to produce a film with Peter? But how exciting.'

'I think it's going to be called *Œdipus Rex.*'

'Divine.'

The Duchesse talked such fluent English that it was almost impossible for Blore-Smith to remember that she was a foreigner.

'And Oliver is taking part in the film too?' she said.

'Well, he may be,' Blore-Smith said. 'He's my psycho-analyst now, you see.'

'Ah?'

'He's an awfully good psycho-analyst.'

Blore-Smith had begun to feel strangely sentimental about Chipchase, and indeed about all the other people at the table or even in the room.

'Awfully good,' he repeated, sipping his champagne.

Glancing round he thought he had never seen so many pretty women collected together in so small a space. He was drinking in this uncommon vision when he became aware that Colonel Teape was staring hard at him. Blore-Smith gulped some more champagne to steady himself, because in spite of his high spirits Colonel Teape's eye had made him falter.

'Over for long?' Colonel Teape said, moving aside some bottles to get a better view.

'Just a short time.'

'Business?'

'Well—yes—at least I don't know whether you would

call it business. I'm really over here to—to break some of my barriers down, if you know what I mean.'

Colonel Teape took a single eyeglass from his pocket and began to polish it with his silk handkerchief as if he wanted to make a more expert assessment of Blore-Smith's appearance than was possible after even prolonged staring with the naked eye.

'H'm,' he said. 'You're going to break down some barriers, are you. And where do you propose to do that?'

'I don't know. You see, I am in the hands of my psycho-analyst.'

'And who may he be?'

With his eyes Blore-Smith indicated Chipchase, who was at the far end of the table, talking to a dark girl to whom Blore-Smith had not yet been introduced. Colonel Teape turned his eyeglass in Chipchase's direction. He watched him for some seconds and said:

'Your psycho-analyst seems to be breaking down a few barriers for himself at the moment, doesn't he?'

Blore-Smith did not wish to commit himself, so he only smiled. Colonel Teape smiled too. Indulgently, Blore-Smith thought.

'You must come out with me one night,' Colonel Teape said, 'on a barrier-breaking expedition.'

'I should like to very much. It is very kind of you to suggest it.'

'Give me your address before we part tonight.'

'Certainly.'

A cabaret turn had now begun. A young oriental in mauve spangled tights was swinging about on a sort of trapeze that had been lowered from the ceiling.

'He's a splendid little fellow, isn't he?' said Colonel Teape. Blore-Smith agreed that he was.

85

'He's called Aziz,' Colonel Teape said. 'We might go round and see him later.'

'Is he always here?'

'Yes. One finds beauty in strange places.'

'I suppose one does.'

The turn came to an end and Aziz withdrew after much applause. M. de la Tour d'Espagne suddenly began to blow on a tin trumpet which he had produced unexpectedly from his pocket. Having drawn the necessary attention to himself in this way, he said:

'And now we will all go to *Chez Zouzou. Allons.* Do you like that, Pauline?'

*'Il reste encore une bouteille, Gaston.'*

When they had finished it everyone made a move from the table and down the stairs.

The second taxi, which contained the negro, Mrs. Rausch, Colonel Teape, and the Duchesse, was the one into which Blore-Smith was hustled. As they drove along he felt someone pressing with great weight on his left foot just where he had a small corn. It was either Mrs. Rausch or the Colonel. Which, he could not tell. At moments the pain was intense. Blore-Smith bore it in silence because he thought that the journey would not be a long one. He was mistaken in this, and it seemed an interminable age before the taxi stopped in front of a house at what Blore-Smith supposed to be the other end of Paris. Above the door was an electric sign, appearing and disappearing, on which were the words, *'Chez Zouzou'*. Along the street were other and similar signs. An old woman sat on a chair outside the entrance and mumbled some greeting to them.

'I'm getting sober, aren't you?' Mrs. Rausch said to Blore-Smith as they went in.

In this new wonderland red plush and gold provided the

86

ascendant note in the general scheme of *décor*. A later hand had added some frescoes on the panels of the walls and door, more than life-size, executed in a light stipple of pastel shades, and conceived in a spirit of complete moral detachment. These frescoes so startled Blore-Smith that at first he was unable to prevent himself from staring at them, but as none of the rest of the party seemed to consider them in any way unusual as mural decoration he did not mention his surprise. This, indeed, was to some extent vitiated a short time later by his realisation of the appearance of the ladies present, of whom there were a great number. A few of these were in evening dress, but many seemed equipped for sun-bathing by the informality of what they wore. They sat about in groups of two and three, and some of them, because the room was certainly overheated, had lifted up their frocks well above their knees. At present there was no sign of Chipchase and the rest of the supper-party. The Duchesse led the way to a table and in a few minutes she was surrounded by buckets containing champagne, without which her background seemed incomplete. Blore-Smith was by this time experiencing the curious sensation of being dissociated almost physically from the life around him. It was as if he were sitting with his chair a yard or more off the floor. This sensation was increased perceptibly by the sounds that all at once burst out from a mechanical piano, which began to play *Valentine*.

'Here,' said the Duchesse. 'Have some wine, *mon cher*.'

'Why, look,' said Mrs. Rausch. 'If that isn't Yvonne and Lulu.'

She pointed towards two girls who were waving from the other side of the room.

'So it is.'

Mrs. Rausch and the Duchesse jumped up and made their way across the room. Colonel Teape said:

'You know, between you and me, I don't care very much for this sort of place. It's Pauline who has these full-blooded tastes. I don't know why we couldn't have stayed at the old *Vache*.'

'Where are the others?'

'They will be along in a minute. I hope they bring Aziz with them. I told Gaston to ask him to join the party when his turn was over.'

'Who are the ladies the Duchesse is talking to?'

'Two American lizzies.'

'Oh.'

'Look here,' said Colonel Teape. 'I think I'll just take a turn up the street to have a word with Charley at the *Bar des Matelots*. If Aziz should turn up, tell him I'll be back in a minute.'

'All right.'

Colonel Teape picked his way through the room and Blore-Smith was left alone at the table with the negro, who grinned at him and showed his teeth in an alarming manner.

'May I pass you the wine?' said Blore-Smith, who felt full of friendly feeling to everyone, no matter what their pigmentation.

The negro said: 'Sure, you may pass me the wine, suh.'

Blore-Smith watched the negro drink a glass or two more of champagne, give a series of contortions with his hips and shoulders as if he were about to have a fit, and then jump up from his chair. For a moment the negro looked wildly round him and then, jerking his elbows and knees violently this way and that, he crossed the floor and was soon dancing with a tiny Jewish blonde. Blore-Smith was left alone at the table. The Duchesse and Mrs. Rausch had settled down, as if for ever, with Yvonne and Lulu. There was no sign of Chipchase.

Blore-Smith had never felt so benevolent. The room's bright colours seemed a trifle blurred to his eye and at times he found it difficult to focus on certain objects that attracted his attention; but all the same he had the sensation of being at peace with himself and with everyone else all round him. He became lost in reverie so thoroughly that it was several minutes before he noticed that someone else had come to sit at his table.

'*Eh bien, mon petit, tu penses . . . ?*'

She was a plump little creature with an Eton crop, who reminded him slightly of Sarah Maltravers. She took one of the bottles of champagne out of its bucket and began to wipe it with the napkin. Blore-Smith tried to collect his thoughts.

'*Tu permis?*'

'Why, yes. *Oui, oui.* At least, it really isn't mine. *Ce n'est pas à moi, vous savez,* but do have some all the same.'

The girl laughed and poured out a glass for herself and another for him.

'*Une cigarette?*'

Blore-Smith fumbled for his case, trying to remember whether or not this lady had been in the Duchesse's party.

'*On m'appelle Yoyo,*' she said.

'Oh, yes, I see. *Je comprends.*'

She took the box of matches from him after he had lighted her cigarette and wrote YOYO with matches on the table in front of him.

'*Charmante,*' Blore-Smith managed to say.

He realised now that she had not been one of the supper-party and he began to feel some embarrassment at the thought of Colonel Teape, due back any moment from his visit to the *Bar des Matelots,* finding him sitting with an unknown woman. He felt that Colonel Teape would be displeased by such a thing. He looked such a gentleman of the old school, and he had already expressed disapproval of the environment *Chez Zouzou*. It was for this reason that when Yoyo suggested, or seemed to suggest, that they should leave the table and explore the other rooms in the house he agreed to do so. He only intended to stay away from the mechanical piano for a few minutes because it was inclined to make his head throb more than was pleasant. He never intended to avoid deliberately the company of the Duchesse, Chipchase, and the rest of them. It never crossed his mind that he could do such a thing even if he had wanted to. Perhaps Yoyo worked the whole thing, even to helping him up the stairs. Afterwards he was never able to remember.

On the stairs he felt very happy. Yoyo was the nicest girl he had ever met and in many ways astonishingly like Sarah Maltravers.

They went up several flights of stairs and Blore-Smith found that the upper storeys of this house resembled in some respects an hotel. An hotel, in fact, without anything to recommend it. The room they were shown into by a maid with only one eye was small and worse than stuffy. It contained a red divan, a screen, and some domestic fittings. At any other time Blore-Smith, shy as he was, would have made a fuss. Even now he felt that this accommodation was vaguely distasteful, but he did not want to hurt Yoyo's feelings. Besides this, the usual processes of time seemed suspended. They had spent an untold age getting here, but now they had arrived matters became astonishingly speeded up.

Yoyo told him about her brother-in-law. Her brother-in-law wrote novels. The novels were in the style of Pierre Loti. He found it difficult, for some reason, to place them with a publisher. It seemed that he had written three novels in this style and none of them had been placed. Yet her brother-in-law was not discouraged. He believed in himself. Blore-Smith said that that was what mattered: to believe in one's self. Yoyo was the nicest girl he had ever met.

Later, months later, when he could look back in cold blood on the episode, Blore-Smith felt that the real mistake had been his falling asleep. But somehow an unspeakable drowsiness had overcome him, even though he could see that Yoyo was putting on her shoes. An intolerable heaviness against which it seemed idle to contend. He lay back and lost consciousness, with his head hanging over the edge of the red divan.

When Blore-Smith woke he was extremely cold. He rolled over on to the floor and, getting up, found his way to the window. Through the glass he saw rows and rows of grey houses with shuttered windows. The sun was rising behind these roofs which sloped away steeply below him. For a time he contemplated this district, which he believed to be Montmartre. Then he turned back towards the room. Yoyo had gone. Through the wall on one side he heard snoring and on the other a whispered conversation. Blore-Smith dressed and went down the stairs. As he passed the lower landing he saw the one-eyed maid watching him through a *guichet*. He went quickly on down the stairs and found a small side door opening on to the street. Outside, the air was full of a strange musty fragrance that he had never smelt before in any other town. He hurried through several narrow streets and came to a wide boulevard with tram-lines. A taxi cruised past. Blore-Smith shouted, 'Taxi! Taxi!'

When he got back to the little hotel on the Left Bank he found that his notecase was missing. There was enough small change in his trouser pocket to cover the fare and he felt too far gone to mind much about the loss. He stumbled up to his room and fell on the bed.

The sounds which had been penetrating his consciousness for some minutes were clearer now and resolved themselves from a merely random acoustic nuisance to the active torment of words and music.

> *Elle avait un tout petit menton,*
> *Valentine, Valentine . . .*
> *Elle avait de tout petits tétons*
> *Que je tâtais à tâtons . . .*

At first, when he turned over, Blore-Smith thought that he was going to die. The agony of movement, the strange dryness in his throat, and the fact that he was still wearing his underclothes all pointed to some sudden and fatal seizure. The blinds of the bedroom were not drawn and the sunlight was playing on his face. The room looked out on to a well and it was from the well's depths that the boots or some other employee of the hotel was, like the statue of Memnon, greeting the dawn with a song. Blore-Smith shut his eyes and felt the bed slowly revolving on its own axis beneath him; from left to right; and then up and down.

'*Que je tâtais à tâtons . . . Valentine,*' fairly yelled the boots.

Blore-Smith tried to remember why the song was so familiar. For some time he lay like this, hoping that the end would come quickly. Never in his life before had he felt in such a state. His parched throat drove him at last out of bed. He almost fell to the ground. He managed to reach the washstand, where a bottle of Vichy stood, already opened, but still containing a little water. He drank this and broke out into a cold sweat. He sponged his face and lay down again on the bed. Later, looking at his watch, he saw that it was nearly lunch-time. Slowly he put on his dressing-gown and made his way along the passage to Chipchase's room, which was on the floor above his own. He wondered with horror what he would do if Chipchase should turn out not to be there. He reached the door and knocked.

'*Entrez.*'

Blore-Smith heard Chipchase's voice with enormous relief. He stood for a moment on the threshold, trying to pull himself together. Then he opened the door and went in.

He stopped, petrified, staring at the bed. It seemed that in the night Chipchase had been turned by some fearful thaumaturgy into a woman.

A closer examination of the circumstances revealed that Chipchase was standing by the looking-glass, holding a tumbler in his hand, while the person in bed was a dark-haired girl who was drinking a cup of coffee. Chipchase turned towards the door.

'Come in,' he said. 'How are you feeling?'

Blore-Smith was unable to do more than stand and stare at the bed.

'This is Caroline,' Chipchase said.

Blore-Smith tried to speak, but found himself unable to do so. Instead he sat down heavily on a chair.

'You don't look well,' Chipchase said. 'Will you have some Eno's?'

'Yes.'

Chipchase poured out the white powder into the palm of his hand and from there into a tooth-glass. He held this towards Blore-Smith.

'What happened to you last night?' he said.

93

'I can't tell you. I want to go back to England.'

'Where?'

'To England. To England!'

'At once?'

'Yes. As soon as possible.'

'But why? There are lots more things you ought to do here in the way of widening your outlook. The Louvre. Versailles. The Musée Carnavalet.'

'No, there aren't. I want to get away at once.'

Chipchase took the tumbler from Blore-Smith's hands, rinsed it out, and began to fill it with mouth-wash.

'But this is absurd,' he said.

'I can't stand it. I can't stand it, really. Come back to my room and I'll tell you about it.'

'Well, all right, if you wish,' Chipchase said. 'Are you ready to make a move to England, Caroline?'

'I suppose so, if that's where everyone wants to go,' said the girl, who all this time had been drinking her coffee and eating a brioche. She brushed her hair away from her face and smiled happily at Blore-Smith.

'I'm frightfully ill,' Blore-Smith said.

'So am I,' said Chipchase. 'Frightfully ill. I haven't often felt worse.'

He threw back his head and began to gargle.

'But I mean really ill.'

'So do I. What did you think I meant? A little food will put us right.'

'I can't possibly touch food.'

'You'd better try a little. Something really tempting. I know a place where the *pâté maison* is excellent.'

'Do come to my room,' Blore-Smith said. 'I can't tell you everything here.'

He felt near to tears.

'All right. I'll be along in a minute.'

Blore-Smith returned along the passage and lay once more on the bed. This was the last straw. He lay on his face, trying to make his mind a blank. He was still in this position when Chipchase came in. Blore-Smith did not look up. He heard Chipchase walk across the room to the window, open it, and take several deep breaths.

'Have you ever noticed,' Chipchase said, 'that after a thick evening it is always difficult to shave properly? The hairs seem to recede under one's razor.'

Blore-Smith made an effort and sat upright on the bed. He was feeling very near the end now.

'Listen,' he said. 'This is what happened to me.'

He told Chipchase about *Chez Zouzou*. Chipchase sat on the edge of the bidet, nodding his head at appropriate moments.

'And now,' said Blore-Smith, bringing the general trend of the narrative to a close, 'I can't find my pocket-book. Somebody must have stolen it.'

'How much was there in there?'

'About a thousand francs.'

'Well, well,' said Chipchase. 'Well, well.'

'Do you think that it was stolen?'

'Of course. Unless in a moment of generosity you presented her with it.'

'I'—for a moment confused memories of a prodigal impulse clouded Blore-Smith's mind—'I can't have done.'

'Well, there it is.'

'But it's dreadful.'

'Do you know what it's called?' said Chipchase. 'It's known in certain circles as *buying experience*. Now you see how sensible it was of me to insist on taking charge of the letter of credit you brought with you. But don't you worry any more. Accept my heartiest congratulations.'

'Whatever for?'

'Don't you feel much better?'

'I never felt so awful in my life.'

'Never mind what you feel like now. You've your life before you. As I said before, I'm feeling far from well myself. You can't expect to feel well after drinking even a small quantity of the filthy champagne they supply at those places.'

A wave of illness, a sensation of burning in his cheeks and of nausea welling up from within him, passed over Blore-Smith, spurring him to profound irritation.

'And who is this woman?' he said.

'Which woman?'

'The one in your room.'

'I've told you. She's called Caroline. A very old friend of mine. Incidentally I met her coming into the *Vache enragée* just as we were going out. That was why I didn't show up at *Chez Zouzou*. We spent the evening together. She's been here for a week or two on a job. She's a trained student of psycho-analysis and she can do typing and short-hand too. She will be invaluable in my treatment of you in committing to paper reports on your state and so on. The additional expense will be very slight.'

'But do you expect me to pay for her?'

'Well, you can't expect me, out of my meagre income, to pay for your own mental and subconscious treatment, can you?' Chipchase said, rather testily.

Blore-Smith rose up suddenly from the bed, moving in the direction of the basin. Chipchase stepped aside and turned again to the open window, through which he leant and inspected the well below. Some minutes later he withdrew his head and said:

'I expect you are feeling easier now.'

'I must insist on going back to England as soon as possible,' Blore-Smith managed to say.

'All right. If you really want to. Mind you, I concur only because I am so delighted to see you take a firm line about matters.'

'When can we go?'

Chipchase looked at his watch.

'We should just be able to catch the afternoon plane,' he said.

'Oh, no, I can't do that!'

'But you said as soon as possible.'

'I'm sorry. Can't we start tomorrow?'

'That would certainly be more convenient. Caroline will want to collect her things from her flat.'

'What? Is she coming too?'

'I've already told you that she is engaged as my secretary to help me in my treatment of your highly complicated state. You must try not to give way to these resistance compulsions. Of course it shows that the treatment is taking effect, and, so long as you realise that, it is all right. It is, however, important that you should convince yourself of the nature of the difficulties you seem so anxious to put in my way.'

'Then we go tomorrow?'

'If you really wish it. We ought to pay a call on Pauline de Borodino and thank her for her delightful party.'

'Must I come too?'

'Perhaps I might do that in the morning and we could fly back in the afternoon.'

'I can't go in an aeroplane so soon again.'

'Really,' said Chipchase, 'you are making things very difficult. In that case we will travel by one of the later boats. Will that suit you?'

'I suppose so.'

'And now you must dress and come out. We are having lunch with Schlumbermayer. Food will do you a lot of good. Remember that I have your interests at heart. Pull yourself together and come to the *Deux Magots*. You remember the café? I showed you where it was yesterday. Caroline and I will be sitting there.'

Chipchase half-lifted Blore-Smith from the bed and began to remove his dressing-gown. Blore-Smith struggled feebly, muttering that he would be along at the café as soon as possible.

'Very well,' said Chipchase. 'I will go and drive that slut out of bed.'

He left the room, slamming the door.

After the soup Blore-Smith refused to eat any more. The others did not press him and he sat back, watching the rest of the luncheon-party as through a mist, sometimes catching snatches of their conversation, but more often hearing the words as if they were part of the irregular buzzing of insects in a garden, the heat of the restaurant providing an additional illusion of high summer. Schlumbermayer sat immediately in front of him, and, although his outline was from time to time obscured by clumps of black spots that would appear suddenly to block Blore-Smith's line of vision, his general aspect and personality conveyed themselves with some force across the table. He was about forty-five, tall and getting fat, with greyish hair and a short black moustache. He wore a black suit, no hat, and carried a stick. He spoke seldom, leaving most of the conversation to Chipchase; but he continually eyed Caroline through thick spectacles with steel rims. Blore-Smith thought that he had the largest nose he had ever seen.

'And so Gaston is coming over to stay at Broadacres some time this summer?' Chipchase said.

Schlumbermayer started slightly and said:

'Just for a short time he may be.'

'I don't expect it will be for a short time when he gets there.'

Schlumbermayer laughed uneasily and began moving about the knives and forks. He had a fleshy face that arranged itself in folds and was the colour of an old document. Upsetting the French mustard-pot, he said:

'Why not come down for a few days at the same time? You and Gaston always seem to get on pretty well together, and I want him to enjoy himself.'

'We should like to enormously,' Chipchase said. 'Shouldn't we, Caroline? But there is this point. Would you mind extending the invitation to Mr. Blore-Smith here? You see, he really needs my treatment all the time.'

Schlumbermayer turned his glasses on to Blore-Smith and looked him over suspiciously.

'It's very quiet down at Broadacres,' he said slowly. 'There is nothing much to do there.'

'Oh, he doesn't expect a party like the one we had last night all the time,' Chipchase said. 'You like being quiet sometimes, don't you?'

Blore-Smith found that he was just able to nod his head without prejudicing his physical state.

'Of course he does,' said Chipchase. 'None of us want to be racketing round all the time. It's very kind of you to ask us. I'm sure it will be very enjoyable.'

'As I say,' said Schlumbermayer, addressing himself to Blore-Smith. 'As I say, there is nothing to do there and so I don't know how you will amuse yourself.'

He contrived to look so menacing when he said this that Blore-Smith was startled into saying:

'I should like very much to stay, but I'm afraid that we shall be in the middle of taking our film.'

'I was coming to that,' Chipchase said sharply. 'Don't be in so much of a hurry.'

Blore-Smith lay back in his chair and Schlumbermayer, still morose, said:

'What film is this?'

'A psycho-analytical film,' Chipchase said. 'Nothing less.'

'What is that?'

'You will see when it is produced.'

'Who is doing it?'

Chipchase nodded his head in the direction of Blore-Smith.

'In connection with Maltravers,' he said.

'Peter Maltravers?'

'Who else?'

Schlumbermayer pressed his lips together and raised his eyebrows. Then he moved his head from side to side with slow regularity as if he were a human metronome. He said:

'Where is it going to be taken?'

'That depends.'

'What on?'

'Several things. It must be, for example, a place where the psychological state of my friend here will be in suitable surroundings. We've got to find the right house. If we are coming to stay with you in the summer, we might look about in your own neighbourhood.'

'Will you rent the house?'

'Goodness, no. That won't be necessary. You see, the film will get so much publicity that many people will be only too glad to have the advertisement of making their house into a film studio.'

'Do you think so?'

'I know it.'

There was a long pause. Then Schlumbermayer, after spitting from his mouth a number of grape-skins, said:

'Look here, I'm going to give you a surprise. I'm going

to suggest that you all come down and take the film at Broadacres.'

He pushed back his chair and, putting both his fists on the table, beamed at Chipchase.

'It's awfully kind of you, but I'm not at all sure that a previous offer will not have to be considered first," Chipchase said.

Schlumbermayer's face fell.

'Oh, come on. After all, we've known each other for a long time. Why not come to Broadacres? I'm asking you as a favour.'

'I'm not sure that it's quite the house.'

Schlumbermayer leant forward wheedlingly across the table. He said:

'But you couldn't have more room. It's an absolute barrack. And there's plenty of space in the grounds. Do come.'

'Of course if you ever wanted to sell the place it would be famous all over England after the film was released.'

'It's not that.'

'Why should it be such a good turn, then?'

'I want Gaston to stay there until all our negotiations go through. They may take some time. Something like that going on might keep Gaston quiet while we transact business.'

'While you buy his pictures and furniture?'

'Exactly.'

'I see what you mean,' Chipchase said. He stroked his chin. 'Then I may take it as fixed that I can discuss the matter further with Mr. Blore-Smith when his health is better, and with Maltravers—with the object in view of making Broadacres our headquarters?'

'Yes.'

The rest of lunch passed without incident. Afterwards

Chipchase and Caroline set out in the direction of the bus which would take them to the Bois. Blore-Smith, on his way back to the hotel, where he proposed to lie down, walked beside Schlumbermayer. At the end of the street Schlumbermayer waved his stick to a taxi.

'I have to see relations in Passy,' he said. 'You had better have my card in case you want to get in touch with me about the film.'

He handed a card to Blore-Smith and got into the taxi. As the taxi began to move, Blore-Smith ran forward and said:

'But this card says *Mr. Joseph Simpson,* and there's no address.'

The taxi stopped. Schlumbermayer leant out.

'Oh, does it?' he said. 'I must have given you the wrong one.' He fumbled in his notecase and handed out another card, which was inscribed *Mr. E. E. Schlumbermayer. The Bibelot Club, S.W.*

'The others sometimes come in useful,' he said, and laughed angrily. Then he banged on the glass to make the taxi move forward again. Blore-Smith put the new card in his pocket and found his way to the hotel.

# 3

MALTRAVERS opened the front door, and, after stepping out into the square and looking up and down it, followed Chipchase up the stairs and into the sitting-room.

'I passed three people with goitre this morning,' Maltravers said. 'I thought I'd just glance round the neighbourhood to see if there were any more about.'

Chipchase examined the invitations in the looking-glass. He said:

'Why am I asked to none of these? And who is this?'

'I don't expect you know her,' said Maltravers, taking the snapshot from him and putting it in his pocket. 'On second thoughts I think it may be better undisplayed. But now tell me all about Paris. Why have you returned immediately? I leave for Berlin at the end of next week. No hitch of any kind, I hope?'

'On the contrary.'

Maltravers listened, filling his pipe, while Chipchase described the Paris trip.

'Where is he now?' he said, at the end of Chipchase's narrative.

'He's retired to bed, and says he isn't going to get up for two or three days.'

'Any specific malady?'

'No. A sort of general protest against what he has undergone.'

'The best place for him,' said Maltravers. 'He'll get up feeling a new man.'

'That was what I told him. The other important thing is that Gaston de la Tour d'Espagne is coming over to stay with Schlumbermayer, who wants to buy most of his pictures and furniture as Gaston is broke and is selling up. Schlumbermayer has invited you to make your film at Broadacres.'

'What in heaven's name has induced him to do that?'

'He thinks that a film studio on the premises will keep Gaston quiet. It's good, that, isn't it?'

'Good? It's absolutely superb. Quite apart from anything else, we ought to be able to get some revealing psychological shots of Schlumbermayer and Gaston bargaining together.'

'That hadn't occurred to me, as it happens, but it has immense possibilities, I can see at once.'

'I shall go to Berlin feeling much easier now that is fixed,' Maltravers said. 'I don't think there is any hurry for you and him to come out there. Give him a long rest. You can have a look round the place and then come back to England and we can take the film with summer well begun.'

'And then I've brought a secretary back from Paris.'

'Indeed?'

'She's called Caroline.'

'Not——?'

'Yes.'

'Tell me how it happened?'

'Well,' said Chipchase, 'if you don't mind a rather long story, it was after we all left the *Vache enragée* . . .'

Although the sulkiness which he had felt during the Channel crossing lasted until the day after his arrival in London, when he went straight to bed, Blore-Smith found that he was soon able to face the world again and that Chipchase had been right in his prediction. He surprised himself by his own awareness that he was in the best of form. Paris in retrospect had become not so much a bad dream as the memory of a refining experience. An ordeal by torture which he had survived. He could see some of its episodes as having even a funny side. He rang up Chipchase, intending to ask him round. The voice that answered the telephone he recognised as Caroline's, and for a moment he experienced a recrudescence of his former horror. Pulling himself together he asked if Chipchase was in, and was told that he was already on his way to Ebury Street.

'How are you liking your work?' Blore-Smith said.

'I've been spending the morning typing out the notes on some of your dreams in Oliver's case-book.'

'What do you think of the reports?'

He could not hear whether Caroline said 'Very full' or 'Very foul', and, not liking to ask her to repeat herself, he said good-bye and rang off.

While he waited for Chipchase to arrive he found that his talk with Caroline had made him think again of Sarah Maltravers. Dimly at the back of his mind he had the impression that all this thinking about her was going to result in his developing a definite attitude to some problem that had been troubling him for a long time. He was still trying to collate his mental images when Chipchase arrived. Blore-Smith jumped up to meet him.

'You were quite right,' he said. 'I feel ever so much better now.'

'I said you would.'

'I'm awfully glad we went to Paris. Really I am.'

'Now look here,' said Chipchase, reaching across for the cigarette box. 'I'm very pleased to hear this, but you mustn't think that because you feel like a million dollars now, life is nothing more than staying up late and gadding about to night-clubs and giving treats to gay women. It's nothing of the sort, I can assure you. You must buckle down to something serious now that you are back in London, otherwise you will soon find yourself getting depressed again.'

'Oh, I never thought——'

'Maltravers starts for Berlin at the end of next week. When the film is launched it will provide just the right sort of mental occupation at your present stage of development.'

'I'm looking forward to it very much.'

'In the meantime we will continue treatment along the prescribed lines, and I should recommend some quiet intellectual occupation for your mind.'

'Shall I go on collecting pictures?'

Chipchase covered his eyes in thought for a few moments.

'I think, if I were you, I would avoid the dealers,' he said. 'Go to the public galleries and take some notes.'

'Why not small shows?'

'You never know who you may meet at places like the Frott.'

'There was something else'—Blore-Smith hesitated—'I wanted to ask you——'

'Go on.'

'There's a woman——'

'Yes?'

'A married woman I know——'

'Well?'

'Her husband doesn't spend much of his time with her——'

'Some husbands don't.'

'I rather like her——'

'Why not?'

'She's often alone——'

'Too bad. She ought to make some nice friends.'

'Yes, that's what I mean. Well, I wondered——'

'Now look here,' said Chipchase. 'I'm not altogether following all this. There is a married woman, whom you know and like, whose husband doesn't spend much time with her so that she is sometimes lonely. What else?'

'Do you think I might—well—become friends with her myself?'

'Ah,' said Chipchase. 'I see.'

He shook his head and stroked his chin. He was looking in better health after the Paris trip, but was still pale.

'You really feel like that about it, do you?' he said.

'I think so.'

'Are you sure?'

'Practically.'

'Well, my advice is, be careful. Very careful.'

'But you think I might—well—try? You see, I seem to feel somehow different after—after Paris.'

'So I gather.'

'So what do you think?'

'Does she live with her husband?'

'He sometimes goes abroad.'

'For long?'

'I don't know exactly.'

'The important thing in matters of this kind,' said Chipchase, 'is to think it out for yourself. Nothing would be more absurd than for you to importune a married woman simply because I advised it. If you want the best results you must decide for yourself.'

'I suppose I ought to have thought of that first?'

'No, no. It does no harm to tell me these things. In fact it is all for the best that you should. The important point is that the ultimate decision should rest with you. After all, matters were left entirely in your own hands in Paris, and look what a success you made of them.'

'Yes,' said Blore-Smith, and he could not help a note of pride creeping into his voice. 'Yes.'

'I must take down a short account of this conversation,'

Chipchase said, opening his notebook, 'because it may have direct bearing on other aspects of your case. When I have done that we will continue the treatment along the usual line. Have you had any more dreams about the Prime Minister of the kind you had the week before last?'

Later on in the afternoon Chipchase pushed open the door of *la cattleya*. Scrubb was sitting behind the counter with a pile of books in front of him. He was a high-shouldered sour-faced young man whose skin went red in patches whenever anyone spoke to him. He peered at Chipchase from behind a pot of yellow tulips that stood beside him.

'Mendie is out, I suppose?' Chipchase said.

Scrubb put down Eden and Holland's *Manual of Midwifery* and took off his pince-nez.

'She will be back soon,' he said. 'If she isn't, the shop will be left without anyone to look after it, unless you care to take the job on, because I've got a date with a jane at five o'clock.'

'I wouldn't have thought it of you,' Chipchase said; 'but I don't mind taking charge for a bit if you tell me what everything costs.'

'There's a list of prices she wrote out for me in the drawer. You're just back from Paris, aren't you?'

'In a manner of speaking.'

'Do any good?'

'I always do good.'

'You know what I mean.'

'On the contrary.'

'Yes, you do.'

Scrubb came from behind the counter.

'Any nice little bits of skirt?' he said, at close range.

Chipchase shuddered, and said:

'You'd be surprised.'

As if to loosen it, Scrubb pulled at his already unduly grubby collar.

'If I had the money to go to Paris,' he said.

Chipchase walked across the shop away from Scrubb to a vase of madonna lilies, and, thrusting his face forward, inhaled deeply. He said, after some minutes:

'I hope, for your sake, you never will.'

Scrubb, who had by now returned to his seat, put his feet up on the counter. He tipped recklessly backwards.

'Not that I have to go as far as Paris,' he said.

'No?'

'They're after me all the time.'

'The police?'

'The hotsies.'

'Are they, are they?'

'I should rather say so.'

'Accept my congratulations.'

'I remember the first time,' Scrubb said reflectively. 'Everyone else always tells me they were petrified. Do you know I didn't give that?'

He snapped his fingers.

'You showed great fortitude.'

'It was just like the first operation I was on,' Scrubb said. 'Two of the younger students fainted. Another was sick out of the window. Do you know what I thought?'

'You've got me guessing.'

'Meat.'

'Was that so?'

'That was all it was to me.'

'Ah?'

'Take gallstones, for instance——'

'No, please not.'

There was a pause. Chipchase picked up Ross's *Post-*

*Mortem Appearances,* and glanced through it quickly to see if there were any pictures. He said:

'It's getting on for five o'clock. I mustn't make you late.'

'Here's Mendie, anyway.'

Mrs. Mendoza, holding several parcels, came into the shop hurriedly. Scrubb began to gather up his books. He said:

'I'm off now. Here's the list of people who telephoned, Mendie. They all said that you had specially told them that you would be at home if they called you up this afternoon.'

Mrs. Mendoza snatched the list from him and said: 'Hell.' Scrubb took *Post-Mortem Appearances* away from Chipchase and shambled off and up the stairs towards his room. Chipchase said:

'When are you going to give that deplorable young man notice?'

Mrs. Mendoza looked up.

'Oh, hullo,' she said. 'Do you mean Scrubby-wub? He is a bit awful, isn't he? Still, he's rather sweet sometimes.'

'No, he isn't. He's horrible. You must get rid of him. Why not poison him? With a scented flower.'

'All right, darling, I will. Just to please you. And how was the *ville lumière?*'

'Not bad.'

'How are you and Peter getting on with your new boy friend?'

'Admirably.'

'You're both so secretive about him. He's becoming one of London's mysteries. No one ever talks of anyone else.'

'Why all this interest?'

'You both seem so determined to keep him for yourselves.'

'Oh, nonsense. He's very neurotic. You shall see him when his condition has improved a bit. But what intrigues you so? Isn't the Commodore pulling his weight? No Nelson touch?'

'We may be going to Paris for a week or so soon.'

'Come to Berlin. It's far gayer in these days. We are all going there.'

'Who does that include?'

'Peter, myself, and our—what shall I call him?—our patient.'

'What about your new secretary?'

'Ah-ha? So you know about her too. You are well-informed. Well, since you ask, Caroline is not coming with us.'

'Nor Sarah?'

'Nor Sarah.'

'I might consider a change of plans. Paris with Hugo would be deadly, I'm sure.'

'Bring him to Berlin. It would broaden him.'

Mrs. Mendoza sighed.

'Don't let's go on standing here, anyway,' she said, and Chipchase followed her through the curtain to the back of the shop.


Sarah Maltravers stood on the pavement for a few seconds, watching Nipper's Bentley, borrowed from a friend of his in the motor business, disappear round the corner. Nipper turned and waved to her just before he went out of sight, and she blew a kiss after him. Then she got into her own car, which was parked a short way from the entrance to the track, and drove in the direction of her home. Her driving style was modelled on that of her husband, but she had added certain mannerisms of her own to this notably uncommonplace handling and she shot quickly in and out of the traffic, barking out little crepitations of censure when pedestrians or tradesmen's vans did not get quickly enough out of her way. When she reached the garage she spent some time conferring with the garage-hands. After they had sufficiently discussed her own car, and also the new Chrysler that had been brought in for repairs that afternoon, she walked across the square to the flat, planning out the article on continental car models which she was going to write that evening. In the flat she took off her airman's helmet, her goggles, her gauntlets, her leather overcoat, and her leather jumper, without which essential minimum she never attempted to drive a car. After giving the cats some milk, she settled down at one of the typewriters.

It was about half an hour later that the telephone bell rang. Sarah took up the receiver.

'Hullo?' she said.

Her voice sounded enchanting to Blore-Smith, who was at the other end of the line. He felt all at once so nervous that he wished he had never initiated the call. He would have rung off immediately if he had had the presence of mind to do so, but instead he introduced himself, muttering that he supposed that Sarah did not remember who he was.

'But of course I do,' said Sarah. 'How absurd of you to say that. Why haven't you come to see me?'

This question left Blore-Smith at a loss for a reply, because he could think of no good reason why he had abstained from visiting someone to whom he had taken so great a fancy, except that he had felt too nervous to take the initiative. He did not like to admit this to Sarah herself, so after a second's thought, intending to suggest that he should come and see her then and there, he said:

'What are you doing now?'

'I'm writing an article on French bodies,' Sarah said.

'French what?'

Blore-Smith could hardly believe his ears. Had Chip-chase been spreading scandals behind his back, and were Sarah's words intended to convey an oblique reproach to him for his way of life? It was only too possible. He began to tremble all over.

'Bodies,' Sarah shouted down the line. 'Bodies. What did you think I said? Car bodies. Don't you know that I am motoring correspondent for *Mode*?'

'Yes, yes. Of course, you told me.'

'Of course I did. It's the thing in my life I'm most proud of.'

'It's—it's a great achievement,' said Blore-Smith. He had made a fool of himself again.

'Why don't you come in and have a drink this evening? It's rather a long way for you, that's the only thing.'

Blore-Smith pulled himself together with an effort. He said:

'I really rang up to know if you would dine with me tonight.'

'I'd like to very much.'

'Will you really?'

'What time? Can you come and pick me up here? Don't come before seven and then I can get this thing finished.'

'Your bodies?' said Blore-Smith, who had begun to feel quite jocular now that matters seemed to be going so easily.

'Yes,' said Sarah. 'My bodies. Good-bye, my dear. I'll see you later.'

Blore-Smith pushed the telephone away from him, and, jumping up, began to pace the room. Now that the step was taken there were a thousand things in connection with offering hospitality to a woman of Sarah's sort, if indeed there were others like her, about which he knew himself to be entirely ignorant. Many of these uncertainties could have been settled by a few discreet enquiries before embarking on such a venture. He made up his mind that this was the last time that he would take the plunge without previously thinking out every detail of procedure. After much reflection he decided that he would not wear evening clothes. He hoped that Sarah herself could be persuaded to suggest the name of a restaurant that she liked. Wild visions of hitherto undreamt-of successes suddenly beset him and he poured out a glass of beer to steady himself.

Dinner seemed an easier matter than Blore-Smith had imagined it could turn out to be. Sarah took him to Soho and did most of the talking herself. He enquired after Maltravers's health, and was told by her that her husband was away for the week-end and that she would not see him until Monday, when both of them were having lunch with Chipchase.

'Why not come too?' Sarah said. 'I'm sure Oliver would be only too pleased.'

'Oh, no,' Blore-Smith said. 'I couldn't possibly. He hasn't asked me, and I'm sure he would be very angry if I did that.'

'How is your psycho-analytical treatment going?'

'He says he's very pleased with me.'

After dinner they went to a cinema. During the newsreel, at a moment when a racing car had failed to take a corner and turned over and over in a black woolly cloud of fumes, Sarah took his arm. She was excited. Blore-Smith felt excited too, because all at once his feelings for Sarah became plain to him It was a revelation. Something transcendental. Later, when they came out of the place into the street, he said:

'Will you come back and have a drink at Ebury Street? I'd like you to see my rooms.'

'All right,' Sarah said. 'But I shan't stay long, because I don't want to be late tonight. I want to get up early to-morrow and watch some tests.'

Blore-Smith was too overwrought by his own thoughts to ask her who was going to test what, but he muttered that he did not want to stay up late himself. They got into Sarah's car and drove towards Ebury Street.

'The nights are getting warmer now,' he said, and Sarah agreed that they were.

In the sitting-room he held up a quart beer-bottle to the light and shook it to see if any liquid remained inside, and not daring to look round said:

'What would you like?'

'Water,' Sarah said. 'A large glass of water.'

She took off several leather coats and began to comb her hair. Blore-Smith went to the kitchen and filled a jug. Then, to nerve himself, he finished off the beer, finding that it was very flat. Now he was not sure where to begin.

'Isn't life awful?' Sarah said, sitting down in the arm-chair and reaching out for *Si le grain ne meurt,* which Chipchase had left at his last visit.

'Why, yes,' Blore-Smith said. 'I suppose it is.'

'It's about time something nice happened.'

Blore-Smith decided that this must be his cue. He walked firmly across the room to where Sarah was sitting sipping her glass of water, and placing himself beside her he put his arm round her shoulder.

'Will you——?' he began, and then he could think of no way of ending the sentence. Sarah in her surprise allowed a large amount of water to be spilt on the carpet.

'Will I what?' she said.

'Will you become my mistress?' Blore-Smith said, very loud and close to Sarah's face. He remained for some seconds looking at her fixedly and holding on to her shoulder.

'Will *I*?' Sarah said.

She seemed entirely unable to conceal even a small part of her stupefaction.

'Yes, you. Will you?'

For a moment Blore-Smith had thought of trying to get out of it and to pretend that he had not meant this at all. It might be possible to explain that it was only advice he was seeking with regard to someone else. After all, Sarah's sophistication would make such an enquiry permissible. The expression on her face had made him consider for a second this way of retreat, but he dismissed the idea at once. He must stick by what he had said.

'Will you?' he said. 'Will you?'

'No,' Sarah said. 'Most certainly I won't. But thank you very much for asking me all the same.'

Blore-Smith allowed his arm to drop. He lay back on the sofa, white in the face.

'No,' he said, at last, 'I thought you wouldn't.'

'You just thought it worth making sure about?' Sarah said.

'No,' said Blore-Smith. 'No, no. You mustn't think that of me.'

'Why not?'

'Because it isn't true. I think I'm in love with you.'

'This is all very embarrassing of you,' Sarah said. 'You really shouldn't go on like this. There are lots of nice girls you could find without making this sort of scene. Besides, I must be going home now, anyway. Promise me that you won't be so silly when we next meet.'

'But——'

'I'm sure I can trust you not to be so silly.'

'I——'

Sarah began to put on her leather coats again. Before Blore-Smith could reach the door she had opened it and shouted:

'Good-night! Good-night!'

He heard the sound of her car going away up the street.

Maltravers leaned out of the window of Chipchase's flat and looked down.

'Any sign of her?' Chipchase said.

'Have you ever known her to be less than twenty minutes late?' Maltravers said. 'It was madness to arrange to meet here and not at a restaurant where we could have begun our meal. As it is, I daren't leave a message and go on, in case she misunderstands it. She's got all my tickets and money for Germany.'

'I saw Mendie the other day,' Chipchase said. 'She seems to be getting rather tired of the Commodore. I suggested that she should come to Berlin too.'

'What, and start life anew there as a man?'

'That's not a bad idea.'

Maltravers withdrew his head and Chipchase poured some more sherry into his glass, saying:

'Livery stuff, this.'

He finished the dregs of the decanter. Maltravers returned to the window. He said:

'Here she comes.'

Sarah arrived in the room hurriedly. She was flushed and evidently bursting with gossip.

'You've arrived just in time,' Maltravers said. 'We've been drawing lots to decide which of us should kill and eat the other.'

'I've got something funny to tell you,' Sarah said.

Maltravers said: 'I'm in no mood for laughter. It's bread I want. Not circuses.'

'Do you know what that wretched little Blore-Smith friend of yours has done?'

'Good Lord, what?' said Maltravers. 'You haven't made him do something silly, have you?'

'I haven't. He did it on his own.'

'Well, what is it?' said Chipchase. 'Don't keep us in suspense.'

'What do you think?'

'Oh, spill it,' said Maltravers, getting up from his chair. 'What are you being so arch about?'

'He's just tried to seduce me.'

Maltravers sat down again so violently that the sofa springs gave a rending sound. He said:

'Goodness, what a shock you gave me.'

'But, I say,' said Chipchase. 'What frightful cheek! Did he really now?'

'I believe you put him up to it,' Sarah said.

'My dear, don't be so absurd. You know perfectly well I shouldn't dream of doing anything like that. What a little ass he is. Really I'm most awfully sorry. I confess I feel indirectly to blame as I'm supposed to superintend his emotional life. But I had no idea that he would go and do a thing like that. He must have gone off his head.'

'What do you mean?' said Maltravers. 'I hope you aren't trying to suggest that Sarah isn't attractive.'

'This isn't a moment for your habitual bad taste,' Chipchase said. 'It's a preposterous thing to have happened.'

'But I like my wife to have successes. It gives me confidence in myself.'

'Is that really all you have to say?' Sarah said.

'What else do you expect me to say, darling? What did you do, anyway?'

'I didn't do anything. I was laughing too much.'

'There you are. You treat the thing as a joke yourself and then expect me to be furious.'

'But I'm your wife.'

'Of course you are. Could I ever forget it?'

'You seem to sometimes.'

'I must really speak to him seriously,' Chipchase said. 'He'll be trying to get off with Caroline next.'

'No, you'd better not say anything, really,' Sarah said. 'Poor little creature. I only told you because I thought it would make you laugh.'

'But I certainly shall speak to him about it.'

'What do you want us to do?' Maltravers said. 'First of all you treat it as the most awful experience you were ever subjected to, and now when Oliver wants to make a fuss you tell him not to.'

'Oliver won't make the right sort of fuss.'

'How do you know?'

'I will really,' Chipchase said. 'I'll make a frightful fuss.'

'But I don't want a frightful fuss made,' Sarah said. 'All I want is that he shouldn't go on bothering me.'

'Of course you're delighted really,' Maltravers said. 'I expect you led him all the way up the garden.'

'Yes, I did, as a matter of fact. To annoy you.'

'But I've told you, it doesn't annoy me in the least. It shows me what an irresistible and at the same time reliable woman I have married.'

'Well, I think you're the limit.'

'Shall I horsewhip him? He's probably much stronger than I am. Those little fellows are very wiry. Besides, he's going to be our main source of income for the next month or two.'

'And so I suppose you propose to sacrifice me to him?'

'That will not be necessary, as has already been shown. Or have you offended him so mortally that he will never see any of us again? There will be trouble if I find that you have done that.'

'I haven't offended him. He offended me.'

'Look here, Sarah, I hope you didn't do anything silly.'

'My darling, don't be absurd. Think what he looks like.'

'Good heavens, you don't suppose I mean that! I mean were you so insulting that he will be frightened away for good? You're sure you didn't?'

'I only laughed at him.'

Maltravers again jumped to his feet.

'You only laughed at him! You stand there discussing a man who is admittedly such a mass of nerves that he has to get Oliver here to put him right psychologically and myself to find him a job, and you say that you only laughed at him, at what was probably one of the turning-points of his life. You've probably done irreparable damage. What happened? Did he foam at the mouth or shake all over or go into a trance?'

'He looked a bit green.'

'Poor devil.'

'What did you expect me to do? Go off for a week-end with him?'

'There you go, twisting everything I say as usual. You know as well as I do that I'm only too anxious for you to lead a life that won't bring my name into disrepute. It's an old name and until my marriage was a good one.'

'It's not your fault if it's remained good.'

'Couldn't you have shown a little tact?'

'That's just what I did do.'

'Well, why didn't you say so at first?'

'You didn't give me an opportunity.'

'Now look here,' said Maltravers. 'I've a jolly good mind to tell the whole story to Nipper.'

Sarah was getting angry now.

'What the hell's it got to do with Nipper?' she said.

'It would show him what sort of a girl you really are.'

'He knows already. Better than you do, I shouldn't wonder.'

'For goodness' sake don't let's begin discussing Nipper now,' Chipchase said. 'Even I know most of the arguments for and against him by this time. Both of you must know them absolutely by heart. The question is, how do we now stand as regards Blore-Smith?'

'Exactly as you stood before, however that was,' Sarah said. 'All that's happened is that he made a certain suggestion to me, was turned down, and we remain friends. Neither of you two brutes are involved in any way.'

'I'm involved,' Maltravers said. 'You're my wife.'

'Oh, shut up.'

'I think I'd better get in touch with him,' said Chipchase. 'Otherwise he will be getting into some other sort of mischief. What a life!'

Blore-Smith now was merely dejected. He had felt so embarrassed when first Chipchase mentioned the Sarah episode that he could only edge to the corner of the room with his back to the light. The embarrassment had passed now, leaving in its place an unbearable depression.

'I won't say any more about the matter now,' Chipchase said, 'but you can take it from me that you acted in a very silly way. A way that might have had grave consequences.'

Chipchase paused for breath.

'Judgment,' he said. 'That is the quality you must develop.'

'But you said it never did any harm to try.'

'Relatively. Of course I meant relatively. It may do a great deal of harm. Incalculable harm.'

'How could I know?' Blore-Smith said miserably.

'Anybody. Anybody but Sarah.'

'But if it had been someone else you would have made just as much fuss.'

'Certainly I should not.'

'Who wouldn't have mattered, then?'

'Well, that's descending from the general to the particular, and to give a purely negative example of this kind is always difficult. But Mendie, for example——'

'It would have been just the same.'

'On the contrary.'

'Of course it would.'

'Please don't contradict me,' Chipchase said. 'It would have been a matter between you and the Commodore. No one else.'

'So you say.'

'And I need hardly add that what I say I mean.'

'You didn't about all this.'

'Please do not try and shift the blame. And, above all, don't misinterpret me now and make a sudden assault on Mendie's virtue when she is trying to sell some tuberoses to a customer.'

'Of course I shouldn't.'

'Good. I'm glad to hear it. But don't take all this too much to heart. The Duke of Wellington said that a man who never made a mistake never made anybody.'

'Does Maltravers know?'

'Of course he does.'

Blore-Smith groaned aloud.

'Don't worry about him,' Chipchase said. 'He'll get over it. It's you I worry about. You sometimes seem almost unwilling to learn.'

Maltravers left for Germany and nothing more was heard of him for some weeks. Then Chipchase received a letter from him, suggesting that, now that he was satisfactorily settled in, Chipchase and Blore-Smith should come out there. Maltravers's job was to continue for another month at least. He seemed very pleased with the way things were going and implied that it would not be long now before he was at the head of his profession. Chipchase read excerpts from the letter to Blore-Smith when he next visited him.

'I expect you will like Berlin,' Chipchase said.

He folded up the letter and put it back in his pocket. For some minutes he stroked his long pallid face.

'It's not at all like Paris, is it?' Blore-Smith said.

'Not at all. But in spite of that you must keep your wits about you all the same.'

'Oh, I will.'

'And now,' said Chipchase, 'I want some more details about what you used to see from your night-nursery when your guardian had the house next door to the seminary.'

Chipchase opened his notebook and took up his fountain-pen. Blore-Smith said:

'There was one thing I wanted to ask before we begin. Do you—is there any chance of there being any—any awkwardness about——'

'No, no,' Chipchase said. 'All that's quite forgotten now.'

'And Mrs. Maltravers?'

'Goodness, yes. I expect that sort of thing's happening to her all the time.'

Blore-Smith sighed with relief. He lay back on the sofa and began to piece together the high-spots of his childhood.

# 4

ALTHOUGH the journey to Berlin had been uneventful, Blore-Smith felt tired when he and Chipchase arrived at the Zoo Station. As they passed through the barrier a German girl, wearing a béret and a black oilskin coat, touched Chipchase's arm. She showed him an envelope she carried addressed to himself. Chipchase tore it open, and after reading the letter inside he shook hands with the girl and said to Blore-Smith:

'We're going straight down to the film studios at Niebelheim. This is Fräulein Grundt, who will take us there.'

Blore-Smith shook hands with Fräulein Grundt, who had light blue eyes and straw-coloured hair. Only her thinness prevented her from having the appearance of a typical German girl in a French comic paper. A Rhine maiden in a mackintosh. She said in slow and very accurate English that a motor was waiting outside. They followed her in silence and climbed into the back of Maltravers's gamboge car. There they sat without speaking while she drove along the wide streets between the red and yellow flat-blocks of Berlin Westen. Soon they left the town and began to pass through fir forests on either side of the straight white road. At one point Blore-Smith noticed stretches of water between the trunks of the trees and the coloured sails of little boats. Fräulein Grundt drove fast, much in the manner of Maltravers himself, scarcely slowing up at all as they went by occasional clumps of dark red-brick villas. At last she turned off into a narrow road and entered a lane that crossed it at right angles. At the end of this lane gates like those of a level-crossing blocked the way. On either side of the gates were lodges, and beyond them, at some distance off, stood a number of low square structures like aeroplane hangars. Rising out of the centre of these was a larger and more pretentious building, a sort of town hall, and beyond this again, on the horizon, the outline of Greek or Roman ruins stood out against the flat blue-grey sky. A triumphal arch stretched above the gates on which was written, in gothic characters, *Niebelheimnazionalkunstfilmgesellschaft.*

On recognising the car a porter came forward to open the gates and Fräulein Grundt drove through, gathering speed to about fifty-five along the asphalt way and passing on the left a group of tables and chairs like those of a café, where Blore-Smith noticed a few of Napoleon's grenadiers eating and drinking. The car drew up in front of the edifice that dominated like a citadel the rest of this film-town. Fräulein Grundt jumped out and opened the door for Chipchase and Blore-Smith to descend.

'*Kommen Sie mit,*' she said.

They followed her into a hall lined with fire-buckets and green doors. Going through one of the doors they entered a pitchy-dark passage and, opening another door at the end, came out into a white-panelled room, full of Louis-Seize furniture and lined with eighteenth-century portraits. A curtain was drawn across the farther side. The room had no immediate roof and looking up Blore-Smith allowed his eye to travel far away into a sombre vortex of beams and rafters, which sprouted up towards a roof, apparently vaulted like that of a cathedral. Chipchase and Fräulein Grundt disappeared beyond the curtain. Blore-Smith hurried on in case he should be abandoned by them and lost for ever. He pushed aside the heavy plush folds and went forward.

Beyond the curtain Blore-Smith found himself in the depths of the jungle. Tropical foliage hung down from above him so that he had to pick his way carefully along the narrow path between giant cactuses and spiky clusters of equatorial blossom. Once he caught his foot in the wire supports of a rope of orchids and fell headlong, causing the surrounding undergrowth to shake violently. This attracted the attention of Fräulein Graundt, who turned and put her finger to her lips to enjoin silence. They left this primeval forest by way of a sliding door in a hollow tree and in the distance, as he stooped to avoid a python that hung, swaying, from one of its lower branches, Blore--Smith heard the voice of Maltravers. It was raised in anger, and said:

'Very well. If you think that your way is right, do it your way. It doesn't matter to me whether the *Niebelheim-nazionalkunstfilmgesellschaft* is a laughing-stock all over the English-speaking world. It is a subject to which I feel wholly indifferent.'

A muffled voice replied to this, but not loud enough for the sense of the words to be plain. By this time Blore-Smith had caught up with Chipchase and Fräulein Grundt. All three of them at the same instant came out from behind a wing of scenery and into the blaze of light that shone from several powerful arc-lamps that were trained like search-lights on to a group of people wearing solar topis and carrying rifles. There were also some negroes, shining and almost naked. Maltravers, with his hands in his pockets, stood in front of these, facing an elderly man about four feet high who wore dark glasses and whose right arm ended in a hook. At that moment, that is to say, the period of time coinciding with Blore-Smith's grasp of the identity of the scene's protagonist, the elderly man seemed to be in the act of threatening Maltravers with his hook. Immediately after this realisation Blore-Smith once more fell heavily to the ground, this time on account of a piece of camera apparatus that trailed in his path when he pressed forward to get a better view of the theatre of war. The noise that accompanied this second collapse drew to him the attention of everyone present.

'Ah, here you are at last,' said Maltravers, turning from his dwarf adversary. 'What sort of a journey did you have?'

'Lousy,' said Chipchase.

'I thought you would,' Maltravers said. 'But let me introduce you to the Herr-Direktor. The greatest film-producer in Germany. Herr Roth—Herren Chipchase and Blore-Smith.'

They shook hands with the dwarf, who, although clearly in a fury, clicked his heels together and offered his unhooked arm, and yelled shrilly:

'Roth!'

'At the moment,' Maltravers said, 'Herr Roth and I have a small disagreement about a point. Perhaps you might help with an outside opinion.'

'We should be delighted,' Chipchase said.

Maltravers said: 'The scene is Central Africa. The hero is, in the German version, a Korps student who wants to be a soldier; in the French version a soldier who wants to be a poet; and in the English version an English gentleman who wants to be an English gentleman. All are thwarted in their desires and adjourn to the great open (or, to be more accurate, the great enclosed) spaces where they each meet another Korps student, soldier-poet, and English gentleman, respectively, who is living with a native girl. They quarrel over this woman and one of them is killed. As he lies dying while the surrounding tribes of cannibals advance towards the hut, the German says: *"Muth verloren, alles verloren, Da wär as besser, nicht geboren."* The Frenchman says: *"J'irai loin—bien loin, comme un*

*bohémien, par la Nature, heureux comme avec une femme."*
The Englishman says: *"Play up and play the game."* '

'There's something you can't improve on.'

'While the oncoming cannibals croon the refrain of the "Boating Song" from the jungle, over which night is falling.'

'All of it?'

'Only the first two and the last verses.'

'Quite perfect.'

'They say it will take too long, because they will have to get the music from England.'

'Absurd.'

Maltravers turned in the direction of Herr Roth. He said:

'You see, this Englishman is in complete agreement with me, Herr-Direktor.'

Herr Roth had evidently had enough of Maltravers for the time being. He threw the script he was carrying on to the ground and shouted:

*'Gross Gott!'*

Then he spat on the floor and hurried off the set, making his way between two banana trees. He disappeared behind a native kraal. A buzz of conversation broke out among the people standing round the arc-lamps. Maltravers sighed.

'It's always the same,' he said in a lower voice to Chipchase. 'He simply can't keep his temper.'

'Foreigners don't seem able to, somehow.'

'I found everything in a terrible mess when I arrived here. At first no one would do what I told them.'

'There still seems some opposition.'

'There certainly is. Shall I show you round?'

'Look here,' said Chipchase, 'we've had a tiring journey. How about doing that some other time?'

'We'll go straight across to the hotel,' Maltravers said. 'Wait a moment, I'll introduce you to a few people. Herr Schrott, Herr Kuhn, Herr Rubenstein, Herr Israels, Herr Bondy, Herr Andersen, Herr von Neustadt, Mademoiselle Dupont, Madame Obolenska, Fräulein von Bernhardi . . .'

Chipchase and Blore-Smith shook hands all round, including the scene-shifters. It took a long time, and at the end of it Maltravers said:

'Come along. We will go back to the hotel for lunch. The food at the canteen is uneatable.'

'Where are we staying?' Blore-Smith said.

'At the Sans Souci Palast. It's a little hotel in the woods not far from here. Very convenient for the studios.'

'Aren't we going to stay in Berlin itself?'

'We'll move up there later. At present it is better to be near the scene of action.'

Blore-Smith was disappointed to hear that they were not going to stay in the heart of the capital, but he said nothing. He had learnt that it was better to be quiet when he was with Maltravers and Chipchase. He would have their eventual move as something to look forward to. They followed Maltravers by another route to the car.

'What has happened to Miss Grundt?' Chipchase said.

'Oh, Hedwig. She's got to see one of the actresses about something,' Maltravers said. 'She will find her own way to the hotel.'

'Will she indeed? Tell us about her.'

'She's got a walk-on part in the Napoleon film. But she's much too good for that. She has the makings of a great actress in her. If she was in my hands a bit longer she could do something big.'

'I have no idea what you mean,' Chipchase said, 'but are we to understand that the lady is under your protection at the moment?'

'I feel a little responsible for her.'

'Ah.'

They got into the car and drove once more through the gates and across the main road into some woods.

'Hedwig might come in useful when we begin to shoot *Œdipus Rex*,' Maltravers said, as they slowed up. 'There's the hotel. Just ahead of us.'

The Sans Souci Palast was on a corner where four roads met. It stood back, half hidden by fir trees, a white building designed on modern principles with a wide enclosed veranda in front of it, the top of which made a balcony for the rooms on the first floor. On the gravel space in front of the entrance were some green tables and chairs, rusty and piled on one another. There was no sign of life, and at first sight the place seemed to be an isolation hospital or a hydro, rather than a hotel.

'Wait a moment,' said Maltravers. 'I'll get Adolf.'

He got out of the car and returned a few minutes later, bringing with him a tall waiter with a drooping moustache and a dark carmine-coloured nose. The waiter, who wore a short white coat, gave Chipchase a military salute, winked at Blore-Smith, and took charge of the luggage. Chipchase and Blore-Smith followed Maltravers up the steps which led to the veranda. Inside, seated at one of the tables, a very smartly dressed man was drinking benedictine. He bowed curtly to them as they passed.

'Who is that?' Chipchase said.

Maltravers said: 'That is Rowland Inglethorne.'

'The actor?'

'He is second lead in the main picture they are producing here now—the Napoleon film, not the tropical one—but he had a quarrel with the producer this morning and he is going back to England this evening.'

'But what will they do?' Blore-Smith said.

'They will have to wait until he comes back,' Maltravers said.

'But perhaps he won't come back.'

'Don't you worry,' Maltravers said. 'He'll come back all right. These are your rooms. What do you want for lunch? I'll go down and order it.'

'What is there?' Chipchase said.

*'Wiener schnitzel.'*

'What else?'

'Eggs.'

'Is that all?'

'Yes.'

'Eggs, then,' said Chipchase. 'Is this the invariable menu?'

'And you?'

'What was the other?' Blore-Smith said.

*'Wiener schnitzel,'* Chipchase said. 'You had better have that to familiarise yourself with an important Teutonic contribution to the art of the cuisine. And, by the way, I observe that the running water in this hotel does not run.'

When he came downstairs Blore-Smith found Maltravers and Chipchase sitting at a table on the veranda. Inglethorne had joined them and was telling Chipchase exactly what had happened to make him decide to go back so suddenly to England. Chipchase was agreeing that the producer's conduct was simply a case of bad manners. Maltravers was reading the *Völkischer Beobachter*. He looked brown and in excellent health and Blore-Smith now found time to notice his clothes, on which the *Niebelheimnazionalkunstfilmgesellschaft* had already had a marked effect. He was dressed in a shirt and trousers of different, and equally loud, check pattern, both garments giving the impression that zip-fasteners wherever possible had been used in place of buttons. He wore no coat. Chipchase said:

'What are we waiting for?'

Maltravers said: 'Hedwig hasn't come yet, but I told them to bring food as soon as possible. She's hopelessly unpunctual, that girl. I've often spoken to her about it, but it does no good. I'll give her hell when she does arrive.'

Inglethorne had another benedictine and went upstairs to pack.

'He won't get further than Hamburg,' Maltravers said. 'They can't do without him.'

While he was speaking Fräulein Grundt came running up the steps. Maltravers said:

'Why are you late again?'

'I could not get away.'

She talked slowly and smiled as she spoke, moving aside to allow the red-nosed waiter to put food on the table.

'I had to speak to Fräulein Levinska. The Herr-Direktor was angry. He caused her to be delayed.'

'The Herr-Direktor was certainly in a bad temper this morning,' Maltravers said. 'I'll grant you that.'

'Do you often have rows with him?' Chipchase said, beckoning the waiter.

Maltravers said: 'As a matter of fact I do. He finds the greatest difficulty in controlling himself. He tore away all the seat of a camera-man's trousers with his hook the other day.'

'Why did he do that?'

'Wanted to draw attention to his own importance. The man is a megalomaniac. Still, we are great friends really.'

Chipchase had by now secured the attention of the waiter and was trying to explain that he wanted some salt. He was met with a flood of German. Maltravers said:

'Adolf is saying that he has been to England and understands English. That isn't, strictly speaking, true. If you will tell me what you want, I will do my best to explain.'

'Salt.'

'Ah, yes. There is always some difficulty about salt.'

Maltravers and the waiter conferred for some minutes. Maltravers said:

'Adolf also wants me to say that if you smoke Kurfürst cigarettes will you give him the coupons, because he is collecting them. When he has fifteen thousand he can apply for a free trip in an aeroplane to Munich.'

'And back?'

'He said nothing about the return journey.'

'Tell him I'll do it if he gets me the salt.'

During the next few days the weather became hotter. Maltravers spent most of his time at the N.N., as the film company was commonly called. His job there was to last a few weeks more. The final date was still uncertain. Chipchase and Blore-Smith walked in the woods, bathed, spent mornings in Berlin, or loitered about the film studios. Fräulein Grundt was usually there to conduct them round or sit in the open-air canteen drinking beer and explaining why none of the better-known stars were taking part in N.N. productions at the moment. She herself would ask such questions as: 'Please do tell me how in London the serious problem of traffic mobility is ordered?' or, 'Does the Youth-Movement still advance itself well in England?' or, 'How good is the chance that the surtax duty on optical glass shall be lowered?' These questions could not always be answered on the spot. At Chipchase's suggestion, Blore-Smith was accustomed to undertake the task of expounding matters to her as clearly as he was able. Meanwhile Maltravers argued with Herr-Direktor Roth, gossiped with the actors, or joined the others in the canteen.

Inglethorne, as predicted, had returned from Hamburg and was now back in his former part. He had received an apology from Herr Roth and he looked in better health after a day or two away from his work. He was a thin man, with hair going grey, who at one time or another had played every dramatic part from Hamlet to the Widow Twankey. In this way he found himself in early middle-age provided with a pattern of behaviour for any eventualities that life might provide. Although most of his time was spent in a *terrain vague* between these and other strongly contrasted roles, he was prepared for farce or tragedy at a moment's notice. Lines from Congreve, Ibsen, Edgar Wallace, Pirandello were always ready. Inglethorne was a man absolved for ever from being himself. He had become very friendly with Maltravers, although they often quarrelled. Maltravers and Chipchase used to discuss with him the filming of *Œdipus Rex*. It was even suggested that if he had time Inglethorne should help in its production.

Blore-Smith found that he was enjoying himself. Sometimes he thought with shame and regret of Sarah Maltravers, but he made a great effort to keep her from his mind. To some extent he was successful.

It was at the beginning of the following week that Maltravers came back from the studios early and suggested that they should dine that night in Berlin. When approached Inglethorne agreed to come with them. After Inglethorne had changed his clothes twice and Fräulein Grundt had decided whether or not she should wear a hat, the party started off along the Avus in the gamboge car.

Blore-Smith registered in his mind the fact that the first place they went to was called the Eden Bar. After that they seemed to visit at least once most of the establishments in the Kurfürstendamm. When they had dinner he was vaguely aware of the atmosphere of an aquarium. Or at least the immediate proximity of goldfish housed on a larger scale than he had ever before seen in a restaurant. After dinner Maltravers had a quarrel with Inglethorne because

134

Inglethorne tried to pay the bill and Maltravers said that Inglethorne was his guest. In order that honour should be satisfied they went on to several more places at Inglethorne's expense. It was about three night-clubs farther on that Fräulein Grundt began to cry because she said that Maltravers was taking no notice of her. Maltravers had just ordered her to find her own way home, when everyone's attention was distracted by the arrival of Herr-Direktor Roth with an immensely beautiful girl rather more than six foot high. They began to dance as soon as they came into the room. Chipchase said:

'How does he get them? The hook?'

'It's mostly bluff,' Maltravers said.

When Herr Roth saw them he stopped dancing and asked if they would join him at his table. He seemed to have forgotten any differences he might have had with Maltravers and pinched his ear as if he had been Napoleon with one of his grenadiers. In the excitement at having the Herr-Direktor at the same table Fräulein Grundt forgot her troubles. Herr Roth noticed her and asked Maltravers who she was. He seemed glad to hear that she was employed at the N.N. Soon after this Herr Roth's partner said that she was tired of this place and, as Inglethorne still bore a grudge against Herr Roth in connection with his recent rustication to Hamburg and had assumed the face he made when about to pick a quarrel, it was generally agreed that another move might be a good thing. Blore-Smith had some coffee to steady his nerves. One or two other people joined the party and the name of their next port of call was passed round. As they left, the band played *Rule, Britannia,* softly.

'Don't get lost this time,' Chipchase said in Blore-Smith's ear, giving what Blore-Smith thought a rather nasty laugh.

'We can walk,' Maltravers said. 'It's just round the corner.'

Two brownshirts were selling papers in the street when they went outside. Maltravers said:

'Heil Hitler.'

'Heil Hitler,' said the brownshirts.

'They'll be coming into power soon,' Maltravers said. 'Just as well to be on the right side of them.'

Maltravers led the way through side streets until they came to a doorway by which stood a notice saying that this was the Real Berlin. The notice said this in several languages, and some highly coloured effigies in cardboard, larger than life and only a little less natural, stood on the threshold, presaging what might be found within. Maltravers, Chipchase, Blore-Smith, Inglethorne, Fräulein Grundt, Herr Roth, Herr Roth's girl, and several anonymous supers went along a passage and into a small ante-room with a bar. Beyond this was another room, very wide and high, containing tables and a band. As he was following the others into the big room, Maltravers took Blore-Smith by the arm. He said:

'I want to introduce you to Herman. We can join them later.'

He led Blore-Smith across to the bar, which was presided over by a supercilious young man in a mauve silk Russian shirt. Maltravers said:

'Good-evening, Herman. How are you this evening?'

Herman's face brightened up when he was spoken to. He had sad pencilled eyebrows and flashing teeth. He shook hands with Maltravers and then with Blore-Smith.

'So,' he said, 'you have now a new friend? That is nice. One sees that it is nice. I knew that you would not always bring girls to see me. Did not I tell you?'

Herman looked closely at Blore-Smith. He said:

'So nice a boy. You will bring him to see me often, yes? You would like that?'

He addressed his last sentence to Blore-Smith, who mumbled that he would be very pleased to come again if he could. Herman leant over the bar and took the sleeve of his coat. He felt the material between his finger and thumb. Then he shook his head.

'The cloth is not so good,' he said to Maltravers. 'It is fair, but not so good as yours. I will tell you. There is a shop not far from here where I find the cloth so good as English cloth. Indeed excellent suits. You must take your friend there. In Berlin, you see, it is easy if you know the good places to get good English suits. Not perhaps so good as yours, but than this far better. And ties'—Herman let go of Blore-Smith's arm and turned his attention to his tie— 'for two marks fifty you can have ties that are so much better, yes, *so much* better than this one——'

'I'll take him there tomorrow,' said Maltravers. 'And now we must hurry on and join our friends.'

'And his shoes. Let me see, please——'

'Another time, Herman,' Maltravers said.

'But yes,' Blore-Smith heard Herman say as they left him, 'it is so cheap and your friend will be so nicely dressed——'

'Herman is charming, isn't he?' said Maltravers, as they entered the big room.

At first sight this seemed to Blore-Smith much the same as the night-club they had just left except that it was on a larger scale. It was indeed larger than any of the places they had visited that evening. The band was playing a tango and several couples were dancing. Blore-Smith was surprised to notice in the middle of the floor two business men in black-striped suits, one of whom wore pince-nez, while the other's head was closely shaved and shiny. The effect was so unfamiliar that he was tempted to ask Maltravers about them, but he decided that he would wait until something else attracted his attention so that he could put all his questions at once. However, he could not prevent himself from stopping and watching, and in this way he blocked the route to the table where the rest of the party were sitting.

'Come on,' said Maltravers. 'What has happened? Have you seen a ghost?'

Blore-Smith moved on and they sat down. The party had thinned out and only Inglethorne, Herr Roth's girl friend, and an anonymous extra remained with Chipchase. Herr Roth's girl friend seemed to be getting on very well with the extra, a sallow young man, thought to be a Russian.

'Where is the Herr-Direktor?' Maltravers said.

Inglethorne said: 'The Herr-Direktor has seen fit to go behind the scenes with Miss Grundt. Not before I had mentioned to him a few points with regard to what are considered good manners in England.'

'He seems to have taken a fancy to Hedwig,' Maltravers said. 'I suppose you lost both of us our jobs by what you said to him.'

Inglethorne jumped up from his chair.

'Are you aware,' he said, 'that you are the rudest man I have ever met?'

Before Maltravers had time to answer, Chipchase said: 'Why, look, there's Mendie.'

Maltravers turned in the direction in which Chipchase pointed. He said:

'And the Commodore. What a small world it is, to be sure.'

'What, do you know that vision?' said Inglethorne, sitting down again.

Mrs. Mendoza had seen them simultaneously, and already she was hurrying down the room leaving Commander Venables alone at the table.

'How are you, my dears,' she said.

She took, in spite of their protests, a spare chair from a table where five little young men were sitting and drew it up between Maltravers and Chipchase. She said:

'How wonderful to see you all here. Of course this is the only quiet place in the whole town. We are staying at the most awful hotel. Too uncomfortable for words. I can't think why Hugo stands it. No one else would for five minutes.'

She sighed. Maltravers pushed his drink across to her.

'Have that,' he said. 'I'll order another one. What on earth are you doing here anyway?'

'Well, Hugo suggested Paris and I told him no one ever went to Paris now anyhow, and that Berlin was the only place with any gaiety left, and so we came here.'

'And now you don't like it?'

'Herman in this place is rather sweet. I just like coming here and talking to him a bit in the evening. What do you do?'

'We don't have much time for frivolities of this sort,' Maltravers said. 'We're here on business. I spend my days telling the directors of the *Niebelheimnazionalkunstfilm-gesellschaft* where they get off.'

'That must be lovely for them,' Mrs. Mendoza said. 'And what are you doing here, Oliver, may one ask?'

'One may,' Chipchase said. 'Although you seem to forget that it was myself who advised you to come here in the first place. I am making observations for my new book on psychology. For example, if you will look round for a moment, I will ask you to note the effect of Berlin on the Commodore.'

Commander Venables was indeed no longer alone. He had been joined on one side by a tall blonde in evening dress, carrying an ostrich-feather fan, and on the other by a young person in a dinner-jacket with wavy dark curls and a precise little mouth. Maltravers said:

'Why, if he hasn't collected Willi and Fritzi. He's making a big evening of it.'

'Really,' said Mrs. Mendoza. 'Isn't Hugo the limit? I don't mind the girl so much, because they seem impossible to get rid of in this town. You literally have to hit them before they will leave you in peace. But at least he might tell that little wretch in a badly cut tuxedo to sit a bit farther away.'

'My dear Mendie,' Maltravers said. 'I think you have fallen into the common error of thinking that Fritzi is the boy and Willi the girl. You should have learnt by this time that it is the other way about. The Commodore seems ·to share your misapprehension.'

It was only too clear that Maltravers was right. While Commander Venables was having a brisk and apparently amicable conversation with the blonde, under cover of the ostrich-feather fan, he had turned away with a look of aversion from Fritzi, who had to content herself with stroking his shoulder. Mrs. Mendoza said:

'I can't have Hugo going on like this the instant my back is turned.'

She beckoned violently in Commander Venables's direction. It was some minutes before he caught her eye. When he saw that she intended him to leave the table and come down the room to where she was sitting, Commander Venables got up at once obediently. But Fritzi and Willi were not to be shaken off so easily. Each linked an arm in his and all three arrived at Mrs. Mendoza's side in this formation.

'Won't you and your friends join us?' said Maltravers. 'How are you, Willi? And you, Fritzi?'

'*Guten Abend,* Herr Maltravers,' Willi and Fritzi said. They unlocked themselves from Commander Venables and found places round the table. Commander Venables did the same, but he looked cowed and sat as far as possible from Mrs. Mendoza, though he gave an occasional apprehensive glance in her direction. Mrs. Mendoza's attention had been captured by Inglethorne, who was leaning across the table and telling her that he had always admired her from a distance but that he had never dared hope that his luck would bring him to the same table as such beauty. For the moment this served to cover Commander Venables's tracks. Inglethorne made his statement to Mrs. Mendoza several times, very slowly and distinctly. His repetition made it clear that professional worries and lack of air in the room had begun to tell on him. Blore-Smith, himself rather dazed, listened to Mrs. Mendoza, who was telling Inglethorne he had always been her favourite actor. All at once he felt someone touch him on the head. He turned and found a tall man with a single eyeglass standing behind him. For a moment he could not place this figure, although he was conscious of a sense of uneasiness.

'Teape,' said the tall man. 'Teape. You're not going to say that you've forgotten me?'

'Oh, of course not.'

The memories that Colonel Teape called up made Blore-Smith break out in a cold sweat. Colonel Teape said:

'What a gay life you lead. Are you never out of a night-club? And how are your barriers? Most of them pretty well rased to the ground by this time I shouldn't wonder?'

Blore-Smith laughed uncomfortably. Colonel Teape's eye strayed past Blore-Smith to Willi, and then to Fritzi. His brow puckered. He passed on to an examination of Inglethorne. While he was doing this Inglethorne looked up from his conversation with Mrs. Mendoza and caught sight of the Colonel's eyeglass trained on him. For some seconds they watched each other, and then Inglethorne began to make faces. He raised his eyebrows, screwed up his nose, and forced out his lower lip with his tongue. Colonel Teape also raised his eyebrows and glanced away shyly like a frightened doe.

'Why does he look at me like that?' Inglethorne said. 'I don't like it.'

When Inglethorne said this he addressed himself to Commander Venables, who had sat down next to him. Commander Venables laughed nervously. Inglethorne said:

'You know, when a man looks at me in a way I don't like I have something to say to him.'

He got up slowly and walked round the table to Colonel Teape. Maltravers followed him, saying:

'Don't be so unreasonable, Inglethorne. You're behaving like a drunken governess.'

Inglethorne swung round on Maltravers. Chipchase at once got up from the table, and, taking Fritzi by the arm, began to dance. Willi, not to be outdone, by sheer force of character and in the face of Mrs. Mendoza's exasperated gasp of 'Hugo!' seized Commander Venables and made him do the same. Blore-Smith, thinking it advisable to follow Chipchase's example, and get away from the table, turned to look for Herr Roth's girl friend. He found that she and the Russian super had disappeared.

'Look here,' said Inglethorne to Maltravers. 'I've already told you you're the rudest man I've ever met.'

Colonel Teape now bustled forward and said:

'Surely it's Peter Maltravers, isn't it? Didn't we meet a long time ago with Pauline Borodino?'

'Of course we did,' said Maltravers. 'This friend of mine is a little over-excited.'

'You call me over-excited!' Inglethorne said. 'My dear sir, are you aware you are addressing Maltravers, the well-known public nuisance? You must be confusing him with someone else of the same name or you would never claim his acquaintance.'

It was immediately after this that Blore-Smith heard Mrs. Mendoza saying to him:

'Come and dance with me. I can't stand this any longer.'

Before he fully realised what he was doing Blore-Smith found himself in the centre of the room clasping Mrs. Mendoza in his arms. He was so overwrought that he could scarcely move one foot in front of the other, but she steered him firmly until they reached the other end of the room.

'You must take me away from here,' she said. 'Will you do that for me? I'm sure you will. My nerves just won't stand it. Please do this for me.'

Blore-Smith was so astonished by this request, and by the tone of voice in which she spoke it, that he could only say:

'Of course, of course.'

'We'll sit outside somewhere for a bit,' Mrs. Mendoza said. 'The Romanisches Café isn't far from here. We'll sit there until we feel better.'

'Are we going to leave all—all——'

'All these beastly people? Do you want to stay with them? I shall go in any case.'

'No,' said Blore-Smith. 'Of course I shall come with you. Perhaps we might pick them up later. It's still quite early.'

'Come on, then,' said Mrs. Mendoza.

Sitting in the Romanisches Café they looked out, as from the bastion of a neo-gothic fort, at the crowd. A steady stream of dolled-up girls—Dietrich, Garbo and Harvey the prevalent styles—passed underneath the café's parapet and crossed towards the spiky grey church or to the other corner where a stunted Nazi with galloping consumption was selling newspapers. It was a warm night. Because the café was raised above the level of the street it was out of reach of the beggars, who were unable here, as at other cafés and restaurants, to approach and stand close up to the tables with bowed heads. This architectural exemption was advantageous. Berlin beggars, neatly dressed for the most apart in gloves and plus-fours, would remain immote for lengthy periods, distressing but somehow repellent from the limitations and Germanness of their methods. Like all their countrymen they were hopelessly technique-bound.

'Do you know,' said Mrs. Mendoza, who had sat for some time in silence watching a child prostitute, with a face like a white mask, passing and repassing along the pavement below them—'do you know why I should most like to have been born a man?'

Blore-Smith blushed, a habit he still found it impossible to throw off entirely, and said that he had no idea. He was more than a little frightened at finding himself alone with someone as dazzling as Mrs. Mendoza, and the course of action he had followed in leaving the night-club reminded him of his behaviour when he had gone to Paris.

'I could have learnt Greek,' Mrs. Mendoza said.

Blore-Smith caught his breath with surprise, and tried to cast back his mind so that he could remember the advantages that had accrued to him from his smattering of classical scholarship.

'Is it too late to take lessons?' he said.

'Don't be absurd,' Mrs. Mendoza said, so crossly that in order to cover his mistake as quickly as possible Blore-Smith added:

'Some of Herodotus was very amusing, I remember.'

But Mrs. Mendoza was not listening.

'The Greeks knew how to live,' she said. 'If they heard music they danced; if they saw a stretch of golden sand they raced along it; if they came to blue sea they swam in it. They were natural, beautiful, free. They didn't live horrible constricted fussy little lives like us.'

Mrs. Mendoza clenched together her hands and held out her arms stiffly on either side of her, looking, Blore-Smith thought, with Greece in the fore-front of his imagination, like Artemis carved on the prow of a ship.

'Don't you like Berlin, then?' he said.

'Like it? I hate it. Every minute I stay here is sheer hell.'

'But why not go back, then?'

Mrs. Mendoza put down her drink so sharply on the table that she chipped off a small piece from the glass's base.

'My good man,' she said, 'how do you suppose I can do that? Do you think I should be here at all if I were my own mistress? Try not to be quite so dense.'

'I'm sorry, but——'

Suddenly, to Blore-Smith's great surprise, she stretched out her hand and took his.

'I know,' she said. 'Don't mind what I say. Why should you bother about why I am here? It's very sweet of you not to have gone raking about for gossip. You see, I really have to do more or less what Hugo wants because—well, I'm rather in money difficulties at the moment.'

'But surely if you want to go back to England he will take you back, won't he?'

'You've no idea how selfish men are.'

'But, I mean, if he——'

'Anyway I'm not sure that I want to go back to England —with Hugo.'

'Do you'—Blore-Smith prepared himself for another snub—'want to get away from him?'

Mrs. Mendoza shut her eyes and shook her head from side to side.

'Sometimes——' she said. 'I don't know.'

There was a pause. Mrs. Mendoza played with the stem of her glass.

'And what about you?' she said. 'Do you like Berlin?'

'Oh, yes, at least what I've seen of it,' Blore-Smith said. 'And of course I more or less have to be here too. But we shall be going back soon to make the film.'

'Tell me about the film.'

'Well, you see, it's to illustrate the workings of psycho-analysis. Photographs of types and state of mind. I expect some of them will be of me. I'm—I'm rather a neurotic subject.'

'You can't tell me anything about neurasthenia,' Mrs. Mendoza said. 'But how are you going to do all this?'

'Well, I don't exactly know just yet, but the plans are all prepared, and of course a certain amount of the work will have to be rather opportunist.'

'Is that what Peter and Oliver tell you?'

'Yes. They said that,' Blore-Smith said. And he added: 'Naturally it would be bound to be like that.'

'Where are you going to do all this?'

'A Mr. Schlumbermayer has asked us to use his house. Very kindly.'

'Gracious!'

'Do you know him?'

'Of course I know him. But whatever made him agree to this?'

'I don't know exactly. The others arranged it.'

Mrs. Mendoza sat for some time apparently thinking. Then she said:

'I suppose you must rather want to get back to London and your girl? Or do you really rather enjoy being on the loose for a bit?'

Blore-Smith winced.

'My—how do you mean?'

'Well, I suppose you've got some sort of steady company?'

'Hardly any—that is—not really. No.'

'Don't you like women, then?'

'Oh yes. I think so.'

Mrs. Mendoza raised her eyebrows.

'You are a funny boy,' she said. 'Are you just too lazy?'

Blore-Smith fidgeted.

'They don't seem to like me,' he said.

'Nonsense.'

'They don't.'

'But I like you.'

To Blore-Smith's great surprise Mrs. Mendoza suddenly kissed him in the middle of the Romanisches Café. For a moment he was stunned. He knew of no words for such a situation.

'Don't you like me a little?' she said.

The people passing in front of the café seemed to move quicker and quicker like a merry-go-round. The gothic spires of the church swayed forward and then violently from side to side. Blore-Smith felt that his head would burst.

'But why should you?' Mrs. Mendoza said. 'You must think me the most awful woman in the world from what you have seen of me.'

'No, no,' said Blore-Smith, 'I don't.'

He took her hand. An intolerable agitation was taking place inside him.

'You see, there is no one I can turn to for help,' Mrs. Mendoza said.

She removed her hand for a second, and then replaced it with a rolled-up handkerchief in the palm.

'Look here,' said Blore-Smith, through his teeth. 'Why not come back to England with me?'

'What?'

Mrs. Mendoza was so stupefied by this suggestion that Blore-Smith was confused and said no more.

'But do you really mean that?' Mrs. Mendoza said. 'Will you take me back? You'll have to look after me when I'm there, you know. I can't go back to *la cattleya* at present because the bailiffs are in.'

'Then will you come?'

Mrs. Mendoza laughed.

'I haven't said so,' she said. 'But why shouldn't I? It might work. Do you really want me to?'

'But I shouldn't have asked you if I didn't.'

'But what about the film you are going to make?'

'That can be arranged later.'

'What will Peter and Oliver say?'

'I don't care.'

'They will blame me, of course.'

'Do you mind?'

'Well, they're both rather sweet, you know.'

Mrs. Mendoza paused for a moment as if she were estimating in her mind the value of concord with Maltravers and Chipchase. Then she laughed again, more quietly, and said:

'All right, then. I will come with you. When shall we go? As soon as possible? We can't manage tonight, can we? I suppose it's too late.'

'Tomorrow, then?'

'All right, we'll go tomorrow. How will you get away from Niebelheim?'

For a minute this problem presented itself to Blore-Smith as insoluble. It came as the icy dip after a Turkish bath. Then he remembered something that Maltravers had said earlier in the day.

'I can take the train before they get up tomorrow,' he

said. 'It was agreed that we should all stay in bed late after tonight's party. But what about you?'

'Take your things to the station and put them in the cloak-room. Then come round to the hotel and ask for me, and we will take the night train.'

'And hide in Berlin during the day?'

'We'll keep out of the way, up the Unter den Linden end of the town.'

They sat there in silence, still holding hands. Two groups of Nazis, walking in Indian file and coming from opposite directions, passed each other and saluted, as if about to initiate a game of oranges and lemons. At last Mrs. Mendoza said:

'You must take me back to the hotel now, sweetie, other-wise you will miss the train back.'

She held his arm while they walked away from the café. After he had said good-night to her at the entrance to the hotel Blore-Smith wandered for a time through the streets. The crowds, who in this town seemed never to retire to rest, jostled by him. At last, after being accosted twice by a tall woman who wore pince-nez and shiny vermilion-coloured riding-boots, he made an effort to collect his senses and managed to find his way to the station where the trains left for Niebelheim.

As he came down the dark avenue of fir trees that led to the Sans Souci Palast Blore-Smith saw that the windows of the bar were still lit up. There was also a distinct sound of singing echoing from the same room. It appeared that in spite of the lateness of the hour the rest of the party had not yet gone to bed. He wondered if he would be able to get up to his bedroom without being seen, and he went very quietly up the steps and through the door. In the hall, where the light was not turned on, he collided violently with someone coming in the opposite direction. This person, whom he was at first unable to identify, took him by the arm and, talking all the time rapidly in German, led him to the bar, before he could make an excuse to escape. As they came through the door together he saw Chipchase, who said:

'Why, hullo. Whatever happened to you? Have you been following up your Paris experiments?'

Chipchase took Blore-Smith's other arm, partly to steady himself, but did not seem interested in obtaining an answer to his questions. Blore-Smith was now able to recognise the figure who stood on his other side. It was Adolf, the red-nosed waiter, who was dressed in a black suit with an artificial flower in his buttonhole. He carried a bamboo walking-stick and a soft grey hat. Like Chipchase, Adolf was swaying slightly. On the other side of the room, where seats ran along the walls, sat a large group that included Maltravers, Inglethorne, and several actors, actresses, camera-men and dressers from the N.N. From this group the sounds of singing recurred intermittently. Maltravers, whose face was brick-red, waved affectionately to Blore-Smith and asked for no further explanation beyond saying: 'Where did you get to?' The room was hot and Inglethorne was giving an imitation. Blore-Smith sat down, determined to get away as soon as possible.

Adolf followed and sat down on the chair beside him. Blore-Smith moved his own chair to make more room. Adolf leant forward across the table to where Maltravers sat, and, cupping his hands to his mouth, shouted:

'Not a waiter tonight!'

'What?'

'Not a waiter,' Adolf said. 'Night out.'

'Have a drink?'

Adolf nodded. He turned to Blore-Smith.

'Not a waiter, Herr Blore-Smith,' he said. '*Verstehen Sie?* Night off.'

'Yes, I see.'

Adolf turned to where the other waiter, a stunted character with an obstinate red neck, was drawing the beer. He shouted to him in German to hurry, and banged on the table with his walking-stick.

'Lazy man,' he said. 'Idle. Bad service here.'

The other waiter brought the tankards along while Adolf threatened him with the sack.

'Where did you get to?' Chipchase said, burying his nose in his beer.

Blore-Smith said: 'Oh, Mrs. Mendoza said she was feeling so hot in that night-club that she wanted some fresh air, and then of course I couldn't get away for some time as she wanted to sit for hours in a café.'

He surprised himself by the fluency with which he was able to say this.

'I wonder she didn't keep you up all night,' Chipchase said, snapping down the tankard lid.

Adolf leant across the table again.

'You are a fine character, Herr Maltravers,' he said. 'A fine character. An English gentleman. I'm not a waiter tonight. I am a gentleman.'

'Naturally, naturally,' Maltravers said. 'Have another.'

'On me this time,' Adolf said. 'We are all gentlemen. Herr Chipchase, he is a fine character. He is an English gentleman.'

'Of course he is.'

'Herr Blore-Smith is a fine character. He is an English gentleman.'

Maltravers inclined his head.

'I am no waiter,' Adolf said. He banged on the table with his stick.

The other waiter brought the beer, and as he was walking away Adolf caught his ankle with the crook of his walking-stick and caused him to fall down.

'He is a lazy fellow,' Adolf said.

Inglethorne, who had finished his imitation, said:

'Look here, Maltravers, don't you know it's damned rude to talk while someone's doing something he's been specially asked to do for the amusement of the assembled company?'

'I didn't like what you were doing. It was bad theatre.'

'Look here——'

'Mr. Inglethorne is a fine character,' Adolf said.

'No, he isn't,' said Maltravers. 'He's a good actor, but a bad man. I know some stories about Mr. Inglethorne I couldn't repeat. And anyway what he's just been doing was bad theatre.'

'Now look here, Maltravers——'

'Do you have some Kurfürst cigarettes?' Adolf said.

Blore-Smith said that he did not. He watched Adolf get up and go round the table, asking everyone in turn whether or not he or she smoked Kurfürst cigarettes. Maltravers said:

'I really can't make up my mind whether I'm pleased or furious about Hedwig and the Herr-Direktor. I suppose it will solve a lot of problems.'

Chipchase said: 'He'll probably turn her into the new German film star and then she will be bribed to go to Hollywood and we will all go over there and stay with her.'

The room was getting hotter. A camera-man began to sing, *Wien, Wien, nur Du allein*. One of the dressers, an elderly Balt, began to cry. Adolf had gone down on his knees under the table and was searching for Kurfürst cigarette coupons to further his aerial trip to Munich. It was clear that no one, except perhaps Adolf, would rise early on the following morning. Soon Blore-Smith found an opportunity to slip upstairs and do his packing.

The Berlin zoo seemed as crowded as the Berlin streets. The weather was still intensely hot. Chipchase took off his hat and held his hand for some seconds to his forehead. Maltravers said:

'And now we will go and take a look at the gorillas.'

'Wait a bit,' Chipchase said. 'Vertigo has intervened.'

'Walking will do you good. Besides, they are lovely creatures.'

Chipchase said: 'I cannot make up my mind as to which of us was wrong. I admit I was a bit severe with him in the beginning. That seemed to work very well. Then he came under your more lenient methods. That seemed to work very well too. What on earth can have made him go like this without a word?'

'Don't worry. Come and see the gorillas.'

'I can't understand it. Does gratitude mean nothing to his generation?'

'I expect he's gone straight back to his flat. He'll soon get sick of sitting alone there.'

'But should one go back at once and patch things up?'

'Well, I can't for a week or two until this job's finished.'

'But should I?'

'We must think things over.'

'I can't afford to go on staying out here indefinitely at my own expense.'

'It's all very annoying.'

'Wait a moment. I must sit down again. I'm losing ground.'

They found some chairs under a tree within sight of the gorillas' cage, in front of which there was, as usual, a large crowd. The male gorilla was swinging on his trapeze, very slowly backwards and forwards, facing the people with an expression heavy with hatred and contempt. He had caught something of the national character of the race he found himself among, and his demeanour suggested a Prussian captain of industry at his morning exercises. Maltravers stretched himself back in his chair.

'I'm not feeling too well myself,' he said. 'But isn't that a familiar face? Near the gorillas?'

He pointed to where a figure stood apart from the rest of the crowd facing the cage. The outline was that of a tall man, with drooping shoulders, who wore a bowler. His pose recalled a minor work of Rodin. The stoop suggested in a too obvious way that he was playing a role in tragedy. Chipchase, who had taken off his hat again, shaded his eyes.

'Is it the Commodore?' he said.

'Who else?'

'Sent to the zoo while Mendie lives in guilty splendour.'

'It looks like it.'

While they watched him Commander Venables turned away from the gorillas. For a time he stood still, looking in front of him at a blank wall. Then he began to trudge in the direction of the chairs on which Maltravers and Chipchase sat.

'I'm not sure that I'm up to conversation,' Chipchase said. 'Shall we climb a tree and pretend we're animals?'

'Let's talk to the old boy and hear about all Mendie's evil doings.'

Commander Venables advanced, staring in front of him glassily like a sleep-walker. He had almost passed the chairs when Maltravers said:

'Ahoy, there.'

Commander Venables drew up slowly and did not at once look round. When he turned towards them it was

154

with the fixed unbelieving expression of a sceptic at a séance, convinced that trickery is at the bottom of the manifestation.

'Isn't it a lovely afternoon,' Maltravers said. 'Do come and sit with us for a bit. It's much too hot to walk all the time.'

Commander Venables moved grudgingly forward towards the chair that Maltravers offered him. He said:

'This is a funny place to meet.'

'Not at all,' said Maltravers. 'Have you been watching the gorillas? We often come here and do that. I think animals have such a lot to teach one.'

Commander Venables grunted. He began to feel for his pipe.

'It's good to meet you,' he said. 'I thought I was the only person who talked English in the whole of Berlin, except the barman at my pub.'

'How's Mendie?' Chipchase said.

Commander Venables struck a match. He said:

'So far as I know she's very well.'

'Hasn't she got up yet? Really, at five o'clock in the afternoon! You oughtn't to allow her to indulge herself in that way!'

'She's gone back to England,' Commander Venables said. He drew at his pipe.

'She's left me,' he said.

Maltravers sat up in his chair. He said:

'This was rather unexpected, wasn't it?'

Commander Venables said: 'Look here, you two, you both know Mendie pretty well. I wouldn't go off the deep end to any stray blighters I might happen to meet, but you both know her pretty well. What do you think of it? She leaves a chit in my room saying that she doesn't want to be disturbed till lunch-time, and when I go in there at one-thirty I find another chit to say that she can't stand things any longer and has gone back to England.'

He pushed back his chair, grinding its back legs deep into the gravel.

'Gone back to England,' he said. 'What do you think of that?'

'I think it's hard,' Maltravers said. 'Decidedly hard.'

'I wouldn't sound off like this just to anyone,' Commander Venables said. 'But, after all, you know the girl. I don't expect her to be a blooming plaster saint or whatever you call it. I'm not that myself. Besides, I know I'm no oil-painting. I suppose I'm not particularly clever either. I've spent most of my spare time chasing a ball——'

The thought of his own honest simplicity so affected Commander Venables that for a few seconds words were inadequate to express his feelings. He could only stare in front of him with steel-blue eyes that seemed to have sunk far back into his head from the strain of scanning immeasurable tracts of sky and sea and refused to focus on the caged beasts by which he found himself encompassed. At last he said quite low:

'I thought she was my girl.'

'Didn't she give you any sort of warning? No danger signals?'

'Only that she went home by herself last night. But she's done that before now.'

'No other men?'

'No—unless that fellow Herman at the bar last night— she's always talked a lot about him—if it's him——'

Commander Venables went a deeper crimson in the face and clenched his fist dramatically. Maltravers said:

'No. It wouldn't be Herman. I can guarantee that.'

'There's been no one else. She went back to the hotel with that little chap who runs round with you, whatever his name is. No. It isn't another man here. It may be someone in England.'

Chipchase fanned himself with his hat. Maltravers leant forward with his elbow on his knees. He said:

'Look here, you are going to dine with us tonight. You want companionship. It wouldn't do for you to be wandering about Berlin after dark in the state of mind you're in now. You look as if you want some sleep too. Why not go back to your hotel and have a snooze, and we will pick you up about eight o'clock and gnaw some food?'

Commander Venables blew out his cheeks and frowned terribly. He said:

'You know, you two are being damned good to me.'

'That's a date, then?'

'I don't know why you want to bother about me.'

'You make tracks for your hotel, and we'll have a binge later.'

Commander Venables stood up. He said:

'I believe you're right.'

He was looking better already.

'In the bar,' he said.

'Right.'

Commander Venables waved good-bye and retreated at a fair pace considering the heat.

Maltravers and Chipchase watched him disappear among the crowd. Then they sat down again. Maltravers said:

'I need not explain to you what has happened?'

'You certainly need not,' Chipchase said.

'Of all the pieces of infernal interference!'

'It's in her nature. She just can't help it.'

'If I ever had anything to do with her again,' Maltravers said, 'I'd do something to her that would mark her for life.'

'I would at the same time point out that you originally

produced him for Mendie's benefit.'

'True, true. However, we now know where he's got to, and we can make plans accordingly.'

'Where does the Commodore come in?'

'I had to pack him off in a hurry to make sure that he would not remember that Mendie will probably be leaving on the night train and can therefore still be intercepted.'

'You mean that our game is to allow them a few weeks of each other's company before we weigh in again?'

'Exactly.'

'Excellent,' said Chipchase. 'Excellent.'

'After living with Mendie for a week he will be more in need of treatment than ever. After a fortnight we shall be able to dictate unconditional terms.'

'And so in the long run everything may turn out for the best.'

'Quite likely.'

Chipchase held his forehead again for several seconds.

'And have we really got to entertain the Commodore tonight?' he said. 'I was hoping for an early evening.'

'I know of a place in the country where one can dine outside, overlooking a lake.'

'That should do us all good.'

'And now,' said Maltravers, 'let's go and look at the snakes. They may remind me of Hedwig and the Herr-Direktor.'

# 5

SARAH MALTRAVERS, coming rather suddenly out of the entrance to *Mode's* offices, where she had been to deliver personally an article on car mascots, saw Schlumbermayer immediately in front of her. He was standing half-way up the steps that led to the doorway, inspecting a photographer's show-case full of sepia prints of the year's débutantes. He was leaning forward on his stick, peering with anxiety at one of these. There was not room to pass unnoticed and it was too late to retreat up the stairs again so Sarah lunged at him with her umbrella and said:

'Seen something nice?'

Schlumbermayer shrank away from the umbrella's touch and ever so slightly slanted his face to the right so that he could see out of the corner of his eye who had accosted him.

'I thought you were a beggar,' he said, turning when he recognised her.

'I am.'

Schlumbermayer laughed and looked at his watch.

'What about some lunch?' he said. 'Since you're so indigent.'

'That would be very nice.'

'Where shall we go? The Ritz? Savoy?'

'What about the Ritz? It's close.'

'As a matter of fact,' Schlumbermayer said, speaking slowly, 'I have a certain reason for not wanting to go to the Ritz today. I think there may be someone there I'm trying to avoid.'

'The Savoy, then?'

Schlumbermayer ran his finger round the inside of his collar. He craned his neck forward. He said:

'It's rather far away. I want my lunch at once. I'm hungry, aren't you? I'll tell you what, shall I take you to Bazzi's?'

'All right.'

'Do you know it?'

'I've had lunch there twice this week.'

'You like it, then? We'll go there.'

Later, over some *ravioli,* Schlumbermayer said:

'Your husband comes back next week, doesn't he?'

'He told me to expect him soon, on his last postcard.'

'Only about this film,' Schlumbermayer said with some caution. 'He wrote to me with various details——'

'Yes?'

'Well, you know about this Blore-Smith being at the back of it?'

'I'm vague about anything except the general idea.'

'Blore-Smith is in Berlin with them now, isn't he?'

'So far as I know.'

'You're sure of that?'

'Oliver Chipchase is still treating him, isn't he?'

'In Berlin?'

'Yes.'

Schlumbermayer's face, as usual the tint of a page from Domesday Book, became in his excitement a thing almost of flesh and blood. He said:

'He isn't in Berlin any longer. He's in London. And who do you think he's living with?'

'How on earth should I know?'

'With Mrs. Mendoza.'

'Mendie?'

Sarah was thoroughly surprised.

'Yes,' said Schlumbermayer. 'What do you think of that? I've seen them together myself.'

His news had made him triumphant.

'Have a *zabaglione*?' he said. 'They are expensive here but very good.'

'No. Coffee.'

'And yet,' Schlumbermayer said, 'Peter writes as if Blore-Smith were still in Berlin. At least he implies that arrangements are to go ahead without alteration.'

'If Peter says so he means it.'

Schlumbermayer looked uncertain.

'I don't want to get involved in a lot of unnecessary expense,' he said. 'I've had a very unprofitable year. One's always paying out. Charities and so on. Constant demands on one.'

'But what difference does this make? His living with Mendie?'

Schlumbermayer pursed his lips together and shook his head slowly from side to side, raising at the same time his eyebrows.

'Perhaps he won't feel the same about the film. He may want to spend all his money on Mrs. Mendoza.'

'You are very anxious to have it taken at your house, then?'

Schlumbermayer shrugged his shoulders. He said:

'You know I'm having business negotiations with Gaston de la Tour d'Espagne?'

'So I hear.'

'Something of the sort might occupy his mercurial temperament in a way that I could scarcely hope to do if I was alone in the house with him.'

'Have you laid in a stock of poppy and mandragora and all the drowsy syrups of the world?'

Schlumbermayer laughed so much that he spilt his coffee

all down the front of his coat. Then he stopped laughing and looked disturbed. He said:

'Surely he'll bring his own supplies, won't he? He can't expect hospitality to extend as far as that.'

'It would be very awkward if he was stranded without any. People can be very tiresome when that happens.'

Schlumbermayer thoughtfully rubbed with a torn pocket-handkerchief at the coffee stains on his clothes. He said:

'I'll have to risk it.'

'How was Blore-Smith looking when you saw him?'

'Ill.'

'Poor little brute.'

'Then you think everything will go forward as arranged?'

'I'm sure it will. When is Gaston arriving?'

'He hasn't let me know yet.'

Schlumbermayer brought to an end his efforts at dry cleaning and sank back in his chair. He was evidently thinking of M. de la Tour d'Espagne's probable idiosyncrasies as a guest. Sarah began to collect her hat, bag, and other belongings. She said:

'I shall have to be getting along.'

'Come to a movie?'

'No, thanks. And thank you for the lunch.'

'I hope you will come down to Broadacres when the film gets going.'

'I shall look forward to it.'

Sarah left the restaurant and, after he had found a mistake in the bill, Schlumbermayer took a taxi to Somerset House to look up the personnel constituting the directing board of some companies he was interested in.

'But I thought you told me that you couldn't live here a moment longer and that the only thing to do was to give

162

notice at once,' Blore-Smith said. 'You did say that, I know. You said if you found that I hadn't given notice when you came back you would jump into the river.'

Mrs. Mendoza clenched her hands. She said:

'Whatever does it matter what I said? Where are we going to live if we leave here before finding somewhere else to go? You must tell Mrs. Pinkus that you've changed your mind and that you want to stay at least a month longer.'

'But I pay by the week.'

'That doesn't matter. She will be only too glad to have you for a bit longer.'

'I don't think she will.'

'Why not?'

'When I gave notice Mrs. Pinkus said that she was just coming up that very evening to say that she would be needing these rooms for another tenant. She said she'd spoken to you about it.'

'I told her the place was kept in a disgraceful state. She was very impertinent.'

'You never mentioned this.'

'You don't suppose I tell you every time I have to put someone like that in their place, do you? As a matter of fact we should have had to go in any case. I couldn't stay in the house of a woman who had been as rude to me as that.'

'What did she say?'

'What do you think she said? What do people usually say when they are angry and know you aren't married to the man you're living with?'

'Oh, I didn't know——'

'Well, you know now,' said Mrs. Mendoza. 'You see how I'm treated. Perhaps it may make you a little more considerate in future. What are we doing tonight?'

'Nothing that I know of.'

'But haven't you made any plans? It never seems to occur to you that a woman wants some amusement.'

'What about a cinema?'

'A cinema? Didn't we go to a cinema last night and the night before? What else is there that one could possibly see? And then we've got to make some plans about where we're going to live. Why not take a cottage somewhere for a bit?'

'In the country?'

'That's where cottages usually are, isn't it?'

'But do you want to live in the country?'

'Do I want to live in the country? Do you know that the only place I have ever been happy in for more than five minutes has always been the country? Can't you see that I like the country? Do I look the type who likes living in towns?'

'But you always seem to have lived in towns——'

'Don't be absurd. I've lived in towns because I've had to. Not because I liked it. You arrange to have your odds and ends stored somewhere and we will find a furnished cottage.'

'But I don't like the country.'

'You don't like the country? You must be mad. You've probably never lived in the country. You feel quite different when you live there. We'll keep a horse and lots of dogs. It will be lovely.'

Mrs. Mendoza put her arm round his shoulders and looked at him in a way that made him ashamed of the objection he had raised to leaving London.

'You'll be much happier there,' she said. 'Don't you want to be happy?'

The moderation of her request in asking for a cottage instead of a palladian house or a ruined castle impressed

Blore-Smith. It was this streak of simplicity in her which he found so hard to resist. He remembered for some time now he had been tiring of these rooms in Ebury Street. If he went to the country he would be less likely to encounter Maltravers and Chipchase. Perhaps if he stayed there long enough they would forget about him and find some other means of earning a livelihood. He said:

'All right. But where shall we be able to find a cottage?'

'I'll take the car and have a look round tomorrow.'

At the mention of the car Blore-Smith winced. It had been Mrs. Mendoza's first and, at present, most expensive necessity which he had had to supply.

'Shall I come too?'

Mrs. Mendoza pulled the hair at the nape of his neck.

'You can come and see when I have found something nice,' she said. 'Not before.'

Blore-Smith hesitated.

'You won't go too far,' he said '—I mean, in making arrangements about taking it—before I've seen it?'

'Do you mean you don't trust me?'

'No, of course not. I mean—well——'

Mrs. Mendoza stamped on the floor.

'Why did you ever take me away from Hugo?' she said. 'Why did you bring me all the way from Berlin, where at least there was Herman, to come back to London, where it has rained every day for a week and I have to live in this most dreary of all streets in the world? What have you done to make my life possible to endure, as some return for my having come to live with you? After all, I don't ask much from you. I haven't ordered a mass of clothes or asked for a lot of jewellery. Not that I expect I should get it if I did, as I never see so much as a bunch of daffodils or a bottle of scent out of the penny-in-the-slot machine. Do you suppose I haven't given up something by doing this? And not so little either. What about my friends? Am I never going to see Peter and Oliver again? Why, I used to get more amusement out of five minutes with them than you've managed to supply in three weeks. And then just because I ask if we can live in the country and offer to try and find somewhere to do it you become beastly to me at once. Why, men have gone down on their knees to me—literally their knees—and asked me to live with them in the country. Sometimes I wonder if you aren't just raving mad. In fact that's the only explanation.'

Mrs. Mendoza jerked back her head and gave several rather wild fits of laughter.

'Just mad,' she repeated.

She stood posed with her legs apart, staring at Blore-Smith, who was trembling violently.

'My friends, my real friends,' Mrs. Mendoza said, 'must be laughing. How they must be laughing! How Peter and Oliver must be laughing! And when I think of what I've done it makes me laugh too. I take you away from them and leave poor dear lumbering old Hugo, who would have carried me home to England on his back if I had asked him to, just in order to live in some poky little rooms surrounded by law books and Medici prints. Well, nobody can say that I can't see a joke, can they? And I don't mind telling you that this is just about the best joke I have ever had an opportunity of seeing.'

Mrs. Mendoza sat down on the rug in front of the fender and laughed and laughed. She laughed until the tears began to pour down her cheeks. Blore-Smith could only say:

'I'm sorry. Really, I'm so sorry.'

Then he knelt down on the floor beside her and took her hand. She allowed him to hold it, but for a time she continued to laugh. He tried to tell her that he was really only too ready to live in the country. He tried to explain, in the manner of Chipchase, that his first apparent unwillingness had been caused by deep-seated inhibition emanating from the subconscious.

Schlumbermayer's home, Broadacres, was about thirty miles from London in a residential neighbourhood that appealed to stockbrokers. It was a large red affair, built about 1900, and surrounded by closely cut grass, circular flower-beds, and high banks along which ran clipped yew hedges. There was a lawn in front of the house and on the farther side of the drive a wide stretch of meadow where the previous owner had played polo. Neighbouring estates were hidden by a high wall that surrounded the grounds. The big bare rooms were furnished for the most part with stuff that Schlumbermayer had picked up cheap from a country club that had gone bankrupt. There were no pictures to speak of. Sometimes when Schlumbermayer bought something that was an unmanageable size it would stand about or hang on the wall for a month or two, but for the most part he kept his collection in the cellars. Upstairs in his own sitting-room, which was always locked, there were ikons in glass cases let into the walls and some favourite pieces that Schlumbermayer could not bring himself to sell. There was also a life-size portrait of himself, so incompetently executed that its painter was generally supposed to have been some art student with whom Schlumbermayer had once been in love.

It was a warm evening. Maltravers, Chipchase, and Schlumbermayer himself were strolling up and down the lawn after dinner. The air was still and the whine of traffic on the arterial road that passed about a quarter of a mile from the house rose and fell in the distance. Maltravers said:

'So that is all fixed, then. We all come down here on Friday and on Monday we set to work.'

Schlumbermayer took a cigar-case from his pocket. He said:

'I still don't see how you are going to get him down here. After all, you've been in London some days now and you haven't even tried to see him.'

'Do you think we don't know his measure?' Maltravers said, putting out his hand for a cigar.

'It's not him so much as Mrs. Mendoza.'

'Do you know her?'

'Not well. But I know about her. I used to know Mendoza a bit. We once put through a bit of business together.'

'And your experience teaches you that she may be difficult?'

'She may not want to let him go.'

'You would, I presume, have no objection to her coming along too, if necessary?'

Schlumbermayer moistened his lips and readjusted his spectacles.

'I daresay we could find room for her,' he said. 'She's certainly a good-looker.'

'In that case,' Maltravers said, 'you may rest assured that everything will start on Monday as arranged. I have already given orders for the necessary gear to be sent down by car. It may not even be essential to ask Mrs. Mendoza. On the other hand your permission to do so will make negotiations easier.'

'Yes, do ask her,' Schlumbermayer said. 'I should certainly like her to come now that I've thought it over. Be sure to ask her. I should like to ask her one or two questions about Mendoza.'

'I expect she will enjoy answering them very much, if

she comes,' Maltravers said. 'But I can't make any promises either way at present. She may come and she mayn't.'

Chipchase, who had stopped walking and was now leaning against an urn that stood at one of the corners of a small lily-pond, said:

'He has probably done himself incalculable harm psychologically by stopping treatment in this way. Heaven knows what he will be like when I start again.'

'All the better from your point of view,' Maltravers said. 'I should increase your fees for the additional trouble involved.'

Schlumbermayer said: 'You both seem to do pretty well out of him. Do you think he would be interested in my collection?'

'I'm sure he would.'

'To purchase, I mean.'

'Ah, that's another matter. One can't say. He's not as rich as all that, you know.'

Schlumbermayer sighed.

'I suppose not,' he said. 'Still, he might like to see some of the things.'

Maltravers said: 'If Gaston is coming over on Wednesday let's all meet and have dinner together on Thursday.'

'That would be all right. Gaston and I are dining at the Ning-Po that night. You can join us there,' Schlumbermayer said.

'Why the Ning-Po?'

Schlumbermayer fidgeted from one foot to the other.

'Well,' he said, 'supplies seem to be rather low and Gaston thought he might meet a man there who would put him in touch——'

'Ah, I see. But I thought he had knocked off the stuff lately. He seemed quite *désintoxiqué* when we met him in Paris.'

169

Schlumbermayer said: 'I hope so. I don't want a lot of nonsense of that sort down here.'

'Naturally.'

'Still, we must go to the Ning-Po if he wants to.'

'All right,' said Maltravers. 'We'll be there.'

They walked towards the former polo ground.

'Listen,' Chipchase said. 'The nightingale.'

The removal van had arrived two hours later than the time appointed, but Blore-Smith had only a small amount of furniture, so that his belongings were soon stowed away inside it. He stood on the doorstep, watching the remaining odds and ends which lay round about him on the pavement being secreted into empty spaces. Van Gogh's *Sunflower* was propped against the railings and Blore-Smith went down the steps towards it, thinking that he would put it in himself to make sure the glass was not broken. As he stooped to pick it up he heard a voice behind him say:

'Why, you seem to be moving house?'

Turning, he saw Chipchase, who with Maltravers stood watching him. It was Chipchase who had spoken. He was leaning against the pillar-box. Blore-Smith could think of no reply. Chipchase took a small notebook from his pocket and wrote something in it with a stump of pencil. Maltravers said:

'If only we had known earlier that you were making a move we could have come along and lent a hand. Where are you making for? Or is that inquisitive?'

'Well, we've taken a cottage——'

'We?'

'Mendie and I.'

'Really? But how very nice. You will be able to go over there for week-ends. It's not far from London,

I suppose. Kent? Sussex? Not, I hope, Essex?'

'Sussex. But——'

'The film starts at Schlumbermayer's house on Monday. We thought it might be better to go down a day or two before. Tomorrow, to be precise. Will that suit you all right?'

'But Mendie——'

'She is invited too. Will she come, do you think? By this time, though, you will have realised that when dealing with Mendie one can't really tell until the last moment.'

'No, she——'

'Where is she now?'

'Down at the cottage. It's a furnished one. These things are going to be stored.'

'You have your personal belongings still here. Your clothes and so on?'

'Yes.'

'Then how would it be to send Mendie a wire? You can spend the night in my flat on the sofa and we will go down to Schlumbermayer's tomorrow. I will run over to to the cottage in my car and explain to her why you were unable to turn up. I expect that she didn't realise that we should be ready to begin making the film so soon. Time means nothing to her. You didn't really realise that yourself, did you?'

'No, I didn't,' was all Blore-Smith found himself able to say.

'Or perhaps you would prefer that Mendie should not be invited?' Maltravers said.

'Well——'

'Anyway,' said Chipchase, putting away his notebook, 'that can be decided later. What I want to know is, how have you been? Your nerves? Have you been sleeping all right, for example?'

'Not altogether. I——'

'I feared that would happen,' Chipchase said. 'You know, it was a very natural reaction of yours to leave Berlin like that. In some ways one couldn't have had a better sign that you were beginning to assert yourself. But it was a risky thing to do. I don't want to indulge in recriminations, but it was very risky.'

'I've felt the bad effects of it,' Blore-Smith said.

He could not prevent himself from saying this. He had not meant to speak of himself at all to Chipchase, but he felt suddenly that renewed treatment might after all be a good thing.

Chipchase said: 'I can't say I'm surprised. But we must have a long talk about all that some time later. I see the van is now ready to start. Get your luggage and we will put it in the car and run it up to the flat, sending a wire to Mendie on the way.'

'But——'

'Have you a better suggestion?'

'All right.'

'You are dining with us tonight,' Maltravers said. 'On us, in fact, to celebrate our reunion. Gaston de la Tour d'Espagne will be there and also Schlumbermayer, so that any little things you want to hear about can be explained at dinner. We're dining at the Ning-Po. Do you know it?'

'No.'

'Personally I wish we had made it somewhere else,' Chipchase said. 'I like the Ning-Po and when one goes to restaurants with Gaston it often has to be one's last visit.'

'Oh, Gaston will be all right,' Maltravers said. 'He's as mild as a lamb these days.'

'Is it Chinese food?' Blore-Smith said.

'Of course,' Maltravers said. 'You'll like it immensely.'

.        .        .        .        .

The Ning-Po Restaurant was a dark L-shaped room, full of Asiatic students sitting two or three together, talking and arguing. Two negroes were at a table in the corner with a pair of blonde girls in front of them. Maltravers, Chipchase, and Blore-Smith were in the other corner examining the menu and waiting for drinks to arrive from the public-house on the corner. They had been there about five minutes when Schlumbermayer appeared at the door and came slowly up the room. He stood uncertainly by the table as if he could not make up his mind whether or not he would sit down at it.

'Well?' said Maltravers. 'A drink?'

Schlumbermayer shook his head sourly. He said:

'I'm on a diet.'

'Nonsense,' said Maltravers. 'A little drink will do you good. Anyway hang up your hat and come and sit down in peace where you can consider the question.'

Schlumbermayer hung up his hat and overcoat and sat down. He said:

'The worst has happened. Gaston has run out of supplies and he was in an awful state when I last saw him. I don't know how I'm going to get him down to the country or deal with him when I've got him there. He's worse than he was five years ago. I thought he had turned over a new leaf.'

'Don't worry,' said Maltravers 'We'll handle him all right.'

'I'm not so sure,' Schlumbermayer said, blowing his nose noisily.

M. de la Tour d'Espagne was late. It was nine o'clock when he made his arrival known by poking his head round the door and giving a piercing whistle. His bowler hat was tipped over his eyes in the manner of a masher or johnny of some generations earlier and he wore a check suit and carried a rolled umbrella.

173

'Ah,' said Maltravers, 'I suppose one ought to have known that he would arrive in this state.'

The Marquis walked unhurriedly across the restaurant, winking at one of the waitresses as he passed the service lift. When he reached the table he stopped suddenly and, assuming a melodramatic attitude, he raised his umbrella above his head and began to intone in a low rich voice:

> *'Je suis le ténébreux, le veuf, l'inconsolé,*
> *Le Prince d'Aquitaine à la tour abolie . . .'*

'You're very late, Gaston,' Maltravers said. 'Where have you been drinking?'

'Drinking?' said the Marquis, drawing off his saffron-coloured gloves. 'Drinking? What can have put such an idea into your head?'

He removed his bowler and, placing it on the end of his umbrella, rested the whole on his forehead, balancing the two objects in this position for nearly half a minute, at the end of which time the hat fell off and into a dish of pork pellets with sour-sweet sauce that an elderly Chinese at the next table had just begun to eat.

'Gaston!' Maltravers and Chipchase spoke at once.

The Marquis snatched the hat from the sour-sweet sauce. Almost no damage had been done. He said:

'Sir! How can I sufficiently apologise? It is the first time in all my life that I have done such a thing. It is middle age that approaches. We lose our former dexterity. Ten thousand regrets.'

The Chinaman smiled and bowed. He understood, he said. Everything was O.K., he said. But the Marquis was not satisfied. The Chinese gentleman must drink a cocktail with him. Or if not that, anything that might take his fancy.

'For heaven's sake come and sit down, Gaston, and don't be a nuisance.'

It took some time, but the Marquis was at last induced to join the others at their table and, after trying to kiss Schlumbermayer, he settled down fairly happily to humming aloud to himself the English version of the menu. Blore-Smith was too embarrassed to look more than once or twice in his direction. The others seemed to find nothing specially out of the way in this behaviour. Under Chipchase's direction food was ordered. Maltravers said:

'Now before we go any further I think I had better outline once more the general design of the scheme that we propose to follow in making the first of our documentary films. When I say that the relative importance of cutting will be even greater than when an ordinary commercial film is being made, you will have some idea of the weight that I attach to this side of our work. The juxtaposition of sharp contrasts will be all-important.'

Turning to Blore-Smith, Maltravers said: 'You will, in a sense, be the hero.'

Blore-Smith nodded and bowed his head towards the plate of food that had been put in front of him by the waitress, not herself Chinese, who wore an unusually short skirt and had long heavily mascaraed eyelashes. The Marquis suddenly began to make a noise that made the rest of them turn their attention to him.

'Chopsticks,' he was saying. 'I must have chopsticks.'

'Bring some chopsticks,' said Maltravers. 'Now first of all we shall have to take suitable pictures of the setting. Broadacres must be shown from all its angles.'

'I hope you won't try and show it in anything but a favourable light,' Schlumbermayer said. 'After all, you yourself suggested that if I ever wanted to sell the place——'

'It will be shown from all its angles', Maltravers said. 'In the same way all the principal actors, notably ourselves, will be taken separately in characteristic pursuits. They will then be shown in relation to each other. We propose from time to time to import certain persons specially chosen for their significance to throw into high relief the behaviour of the protagonists.'

'Look here,' said Schlumbermayer, 'you never said anything about these additional people.'

Maltravers raised slightly his hand.

'On the contrary,' he said, 'if you think back you will find that I most certainly did and in one case at least you were very much in favour of her coming over.'

'I don't seem to remember it,' Schlumbermayer said, but he showed no signs of active opposition.

Maltravers said: 'Perhaps the most important feature of the whole experiment—for we must confess it is at present only an experiment—will be the shooting of situations that arise quite fortuitously. Naturally these may occur during the preliminary studies of each character and everything will be subordinated to taking as many of these as possible. *Montage* will do the rest.'

'I will now,' said Chipchase, 'say a few words about the side of the production which will be under my own management. That is to say the psycho-analytical——'

He was interrupted by a shout from M. de la Tour d'Espagne:

'Why do you look at me?'

It was a yell, a sound like a clap of thunder. The Marquis, who until a few moments before had been crooning happily, had half risen and seized the edge of the table with both hands, dragging the cloth towards him, so that Schlumbermayer's food was jerked violently from him at the very moment when he was making an effort to transport some of it to his mouth. The attention of everyone was in this way directed to the table where the negroes and their girls sat, because it was on them that the Marquis's now bulging eyes were fixed.

'What are you looking at?' he repeated, almost as loudly as before. 'Why the hell have you the impertinence to stare so at me?'

The nearer negro began to roll his eyes horribly. He shouted back:

'What do you say to me?'

The Marquis let go of the table-cloth, knocking two glasses to the floor, and getting up began to push back his chair.

'What do I say?' he said. 'I say that the blood of Bayard flows in my veins and I am telling you that I won't be looked at like that by a black man. A black man! A black man!'

The further negro now jumped up too. In a very refined voice he chattered:

'What you mean, black man? Don't you think I'm as good as you, you poor thing, you——'

'Oh stow it, Oscar,' said one of the blonde girls. 'Don't take any notice of his common talk.'

The Marquis had by this time reached the table where the negroes sat.

'Listen,' he said. 'I will pay you a compliment that will surprise you. My second will call on you tomorrow when you tell me your address. Think how fine a death it will be for you, a black man, to be shot by one——' He broke off and turned to the Chinese in whose sour-sweet sauce he had dropped his hat. 'Sir, will you do me an honour? Will you be my second? It is in the interests of the civilised races of the world——'

By this time Maltravers and Chipchase had risen also and

both laid hands on the Marquis. Maltravers said:

'Gaston, for goodness' sake——'

The Marquis shook them off. His face was as white as chalk.

'*Lâche!*' he yelled. 'You coward black man! Booby!'

Schlumbermayer sat very still with a faint acid smile on his face. He watched the scene, but all the time he messed about with his fork the food on the plate before him. Blore-Smith did not know what to do. For the first time in his experience Maltravers and Chipchase, like Frankenstein, seemed unable to control this creature of their own contriving. Both negroes now stood shoulder-to-shoulder and jabbered in unison. The other blonde began to powder her nose. The owner of the restaurant, a small Chinese, almost a dwarf, had now joined the combatants. The Marquis stretched out his hand towards the hook on which his umbrella hung. At this moment the situation was taken in hand with extreme violence by the waitress with the long eyelashes. She took M. de la Tour d'Espagne by the arm and said:

'Out! Go on, out you get!'

The Marquis turned and, seeing her, was so taken aback that at first she was able to drag him half-way down the room towards the door.

'Out you get, you!' she said.

The Marquis suddenly jerked himself away from her. He snatched his bowler and umbrella from the wall, leant forward and gave her a smacking kiss, ran towards the door, where he paused for a moment and shouted: '*Merde!*' Then he bowed and disappeared into the street. All this happened so quickly that at first Blore-Smith could scarcely collate in his mind the sequence of events. When his brain cleared a little he saw that Chipchase was offering his cigarette-case to the negroes, while Maltravers was quieting down the owner of the restaurant. After a while they came back to the table. Schlumbermayer said:

'Shall we ever see him again?'

Maltravers said: 'I wonder whether we ought to go out and have a look for him. I don't expect he's gone far.'

'Let's see what we can do,' Chipchase said. 'Personally I don't want a Chinese meal much after all this.'

'Do you want me to come too?' Schlumbermayer said.

Maltravers said: 'Not unless you want to specially. Why don't both of you finish your dinners and then come up to my flat? Sarah will be there even if we haven't arrived yet. We'll have a look for Gaston and bring him along. Of course he may have gone for good, in which case we'll have to discuss ways and means without him.'

Blore-Smith, not liking the idea of having to force his way in on Sarah in the company of Schlumbermayer and thinking of the explanations he would have to give, tried to protest, but before he was able to take any practical steps to avoid this Maltravers and Chipchase had left the room and he was alone with Schlumbermayer. He noticed that the negroes and blonde girls had settled down to quarrelling among themselves. Schlumbermayer, who had for some time now turned his attention to his food, looked up.

'Silly, isn't it?' he said at last, fixing Blore-Smith through the thick lenses of his spectacles.

'Yes, isn't it?' Blore-Smith said.

They went to the Maltravers' flat by bus, each paying his own fare. Blore-Smith did not speak much because he felt shaken after the scene in the Ning-Po and Schlumbermayer, as usual, had little to offer in the way of conversation. Sarah herself opened the door on their arrival. She was clearly surprised to see them together. To Blore-Smith's relief

Schlumbermayer gave some explanation of what had happened.

'Come in anyway,' Sarah said, after she had heard something of the story of M. de la Tour d'Espagne's behaviour, 'and tell me the rest upstairs.'

Outside in the street Blore-Smith had forgotten his earlier fears of embarrassment at meeting Sarah again. On the threshold of the flat these returned in an aggravated form. He sat down on one of the steel chairs, wondering what to say. Schlumbermayer made his way round the flat, examining everything, sometimes unhooking a picture from the wall and looking at its back, and turning up pieces of china or silver to inspect the mark on each. Sarah sat down beside Blore-Smith.

'What sort of a time did you have in Germany?' she said. 'Did you meet any nice girls?'

'Well, there was a Miss Grundt——' Blore-Smith began, and then broke off, remembering that he could not very well tell Sarah of Fräulein Grundt without supplying at the same time a certain amount of compromising information about Maltravers.

'Oh yes,' Sarah said, 'but she was Peter's girl surely? Not yours? He wrote me all about her.'

'Well, I suppose she was in a way. But I mean I used to see a good deal of her too—not in the same way, of course—that is, I mean, we all went about a lot together all the time.'

'I don't want to hear about her. The brute!'

'No, of course not, naturally, at least——'

Schlumbermayer came heavily across the room holding a mug in his hand.

'This seems quite good pewter,' he said. 'Where did you get it?'

While Sarah was explaining the mug's history the door

opened and Maltravers came in, followed by Chipchase and M. de la Tour d'Espagne.

'Why, Gaston,' Sarah said. 'What ages since we've met.'

The Marquis kissed her hand. He seemed considerably cowed. After he had said a few words to Sarah, almost in an undertone, he turned to Blore-Smith and Schlumbermayer and said:

'Before I do anything I must apologise to you for what happened at the restaurant Ning-Po. I get very excited sometimes. I am afraid that this happened tonight. You must accept my apologies and regrets. Will you?'

Blore-Smith and Schlumbermayer said that they would. The Marquis sat down at Sarah's invitation. He seemed, Blore-Smith was glad to notice, thoroughly exhausted. Chipchase said:

'I will now tell you something about the psycho-analytical side of the film. As I was about to when interrupted.'

He looked meaningly at the Marquis, who turned his eyes away. Maltravers said:

'Have we got any biscuits or anything of the sort in the house? We were forced to make rather a scrappy dinner.'

Chipchase said: 'The film is to be called *Œdipus Rex* for the obvious reason that a great deal of it will illustrate the practical workings of the œdipus-complex.'

He glanced at Blore-Smith, whose attention was at that moment distracted by the telephone bell. Maltravers took up the receiver.

'Hullo?' he said.

Chipchase stopped talking and watched the telephone grudgingly.

'Who is that speaking?' Maltravers said; and then, handing the receiver to Sarah, said:

'It's Nipper.'

'Nonsense,' Sarah said. 'It can't be.'

'I tell you it is.'

She took the receiver from him and said:

'Hullo?'

Someone at the other end of the line talked for some minutes while Sarah answered 'Yes' or 'No'. The others listened in silence. At last Sarah said:

'I must say good-bye now. See you on Wednesday.'

She hung up the receiver.

'So it was Nipper?' Maltravers said.

'No, of course it wasn't.'

'But I recognised his voice.'

'It's quite different.'

'Who was that, then?'

'He's called Chummy.'

'Is he, indeed?'

'You've met him.'

'I thought the name seemed familiar,' Maltravers said.

However, in spite of the name's familiarity, Maltravers did not seem entirely pleased and he sighed deeply. Beyond this he made no comment. Chipchase said:

'Shall I go on?'

'Yes,' said Maltravers. 'But what about those biscuits, Sarah? Surely we've got something to eat in the house?'

'I'll try and find something,' Sarah said.

She went out of the room. Chipchase said:

'As to the psycho-analytical side——'

M. de la Tour d'Espagne, who had up to now been listening quietly enough, at last began to show signs of agitation. Chipchase broke off in the middle of his sentence.

'What is it, Gaston?' he said.

The Marquis said: 'What is all this you are talking about? I don't understand. What is happening?'

'The film.'

'But I don't understand.'

182

The Marquis began to whimper. Chipchase said:

'It's the film, Gaston. The film we told you about. It will amuse you. It's all about psycho-analysis.'

'Le psychanalyse?'

'Oui.'

'But I don't understand,' the Marquis said in a broken voice. 'What have I got to do? What is it all about? Why have you brought me here?'

He began to cry gently in a small silk pocket handkerchief. Maltravers said:

'Cheer up, Gaston. What's the matter? You won't have to do anything. All you need do is to watch us make the film while you stay comfortably at Broadacres.'

The Marquis's sobs became louder and louder. His body shook all over. He was now definitely howling.

'I don't understand. I can't understand all about the film. What am I meant to do?'

Chipchase said: 'Look, Gaston. Here's Sarah with some chocolate biscuits. Have a biscuit. You'll feel much better.'

'What's happened?' Sarah said.

Maltravers said: 'Gaston's feeling a bit off colour. I think he'd really better go back to bed.'

'I'll see him home,' Schlumbermayer said, and added to Chipchase:

'You go my way, don't you? Perhaps you could come with us and lend a hand?'

'All right,' Chipchase said. 'Where's he staying? With you? Are you going back to Broadacres tonight?'

'At the moment he's in a furnished flat in the Jermyn Street part of the world.'

'What an extraordinary thing to do,' Sarah said. 'But how like Gaston.'

'I'm at my club. I'm not going back to the country until

tomorrow, so I can't do anything about him,' Schlumbermayer said.

'Well, we'll see him home,' Chipchase said, 'and try to
fix him up for the night.'

Schlumbermayer added in a low voice, as if someone
might be listening at the door: 'I believe there's someone
in a neighbouring flat who might be able to assist as
regards——'

'We'll find out about that when we get there,' Chipchase
said. 'Now come along, Gaston. Bedtime.'

The Marquis was by now lying on his face on the sofa,
heaving spasmodically. He was crying loudly and aimlessly
like a child who has forgotten the original cause of its grief.
He gulped noisily when Chipchase spoke to him.

'Cheer up, Gaston,' Maltravers said, and, taking out his
handkerchief, wiped away some of the Marquis's tears.

They took him by the arm and he made no objection to
being led out of the room after he had once more kissed
Sarah's hand. Schlumbermayer said:

'Wait a moment, let me see if I've got enough money for
the taxi.'

Maltravers took Schlumbermayer gently by the shoulder
and pushed him from the room, saying as he did so:

'You'll find you've got enough. Take my word for it.'

'Well, good-night all,' said Chipchase, 'and you will pick
me up tomorrow and we'll all go down to Broadacres
together.'

He followed them out of the room. Maltravers heaved a
sigh and sat down on the sofa. Sarah said to Blore-Smith:
'If you are staying here tonight we must begin trying to
fix you up with a bed. We might start by moving some of
the typewriters.'

After passing an only moderately comfortable night on

the sofa Blore-Smith had breakfast with Maltravers alone, as they were making an early start and Sarah had decided to stay in bed until later in the day. During this meal Maltravers spoke on the subject of the Marquis de la Tour d'Espagne.

'Gaston has far too much energy,' he said. 'Nothing short of world upheaval provides sufficient occupation for him. During the war, for example, he did well. In fact I attribute much of his subsequent behaviour to the fact that his war record was so good. I suppose he feels subconsciously that if he kicks up enough fuss war will break out again as a result.'

'But he was quite all right when I first met him,' Blore-Smith said.

Maltravers said: 'He has his quiet periods. And of course opium is a great preservative. When it's scarce he raises hell. But come along now. We must start.'

They drove in the yellow car towards Bloomsbury, where they were picking up Chipchase. He was looking out of his window when they arrived and soon joined them with his suitcase. Maltravers said:

'Did you get Gaston back all right last night?'

'He seemed fairly happy by the time we left him,' Chipchase said. 'And Schlumbermayer rang me up this morning to say that he's arranged to have a twist of Gaston's favourite baccy at Broadacres when he arrives, so that should be an additional inducement to get him there.'

'That's very handsome of him.'

'He says that Gaston has to make his own arrangements in future, but he understands that it wasn't altogether Gaston's fault that he was left short this time.'

Maltravers said: 'You know, this deal Schlumbermayer hopes to put through must be pretty important for him to take all this trouble.'

Chipchase said: 'I always knew Gaston had inherited some very nice things.'

The car drew up in front of the entrance to a small block of flats. Chipchase said:

'I think I'll wait down here. I had enough of Gaston last night to satisfy me for some time.'

'Shall I wait too?' Blore-Smith said.

'You go up,' Chipchase said. 'It may prove very instructive.'

Blore-Smith followed Maltravers into the lift and they went up several floors. Maltravers said:

'What a place to live.'

He rang the bell of a door with frosted-glass panels at the end of a small passage. The door was opened by a charwoman, a depressed character, so over-equipped with the traditional badges of her profession that she had the air of an amateur stage-impersonator. Maltravers said:

'Is the Marquis in?'

The old woman did not speak, but pointed to the door on the left and nodded her head. As she did this several screeching sounds came from the farther side. Isolated, creaking notes, as from some creature in pain. Blore-Smith felt his heart jump. Maltravers raised his eyebrows and tapped on the door. There was no answer beyond a weaker repetition of the same noises. Maltravers tapped again. There was silence for a moment.

'Who is that?' a voice said.

'It's the younger generation,' Maltravers said, 'knocking on the door.'

Another confused burst of sound came from the next room. Maltravers turned the handle of the door and Blore-Smith followed him across the threshold.

'My dear Gaston,' Blore-Smith heard Maltravers say.

The Marquis was sitting on the window-seat with a coaching-horn in his hand. He continued to make unsuccessful efforts to blow this and merely waved to them with his left hand as an acknowledgment of their arrival. There was a bottle of yellow chartreuse on the table beside him. The air was charged with a musty sweetish smell. Maltravers said:

'Is this your latest hobby?'

Blore-Smith looked round the room. It was furnished with heavy leather arm-chairs and had a brown and gold embossed wallpaper. Lace curtains kept out some of the sun, but a few shafts of light fell on a boule cabinet on which stood an eastern maiden done in bronze, holding a lamp. Maltravers said:

'Let's hear the Last Post.'

Suddenly the Marquis jumped up from where he was sitting. He threw the coaching-horn to the floor. Grasping Blore-Smith by the hands he began to dance round the room with him. Blore-Smith was unprepared for anything of this sort and found himself dragged round and round and round in a dizzy whirl, while the Marquis began to sing:

> *'We are two funny men,*
> *The funniest ever seen,*
> *And one is Mr. Gallagher,*
> *And one is Mr. Sheen . . .'*

After a few moments Blore-Smith lost his balance and fell heavily to the floor. The Marquis, breathless, returned to his place in the window-seat. Maltravers said:

'I suppose you haven't packed, Gaston? You know we are off to Schlumbermayer's this morning.'

The Marquis, who had begun to study with great concentration a newspaper that lay beside him, looked up. He pushed the paper across the table in the direction of Maltravers and pointed to a square at the bottom of the page which was divided up into eight compartments, each of which contained a small picture depicting two or more objects.

'They are railway stations,' the Marquis said. 'I've got most of them. All the easy ones, in fact. Basingstoke. Horsham. Leeds. Aberdeen. But this lion and the church. It seems impossible. Is there a town Lionchurch? You see, it is vitally important that I win this. Let me read out some of the prizes to you. The first prize: a two-seater car. Second prize: a radiogramophone. Third prize: a tandem bicycle. Now what I want is the *third prize*. Do you think, Peter, that if I win the first prize they will allow me to choose the third prize? You see, if I can only get this picture of the lion and the church I am certain to win it. What do you think?'

Maltravers said: 'Gaston. If I tell you what that picture is will you promise to pack your things and come quietly to Schlumbermayer's?'

The Marquis looked uncertain.

'What do you think?' he said. 'If I win will they let me have the third prize?'

'Of course they will.'

'What is it, then?'

'Do you promise to come?'

'*Et bien?*'

'Leominster.'

'What?'

'Leo means lion: minster, a cathedral.'

Maltravers spelt it. The Marquis wrote the name down laboriously.

'Now it's a certainty,' he said. 'Provided they see reason about the third prize.'

'And now you must go and pack.'

'But——'

'Gaston!'

'*Je vous demande un peu——*'

'Please, Gaston. You have given your word.'

The Marquis laughed and went to the door. They heard him giving orders to the old woman to pack a suitcase. When he came back to the room Maltravers said:

'Why do you want a bicycle-made-for-two?'

'That's my secret,' the Marquis said.

He went across to the radio which stood in the corner of the room and began to fiddle about with the controls. A voice began to speak:

'. . . Then wrote Rehum the chancellor, and Shimshai the scribe, and the rest of their companions, the Dinaites, the Apharsathchites, the Tarpelites, the Apharsites, the Archevites, the Babylonians, the Susanchites, the Dehavites, and the Elamites . . .'

The voice broke off sharply.

'Sunday morning,' the Marquis said, and switched over the wireless to a man reading out numbers in an unknown language.

'It's hopeless,' he said. 'Never anything one wants to hear on the damned thing.'

He sat down again, his face working.

'And then my pipe has disappeared too,' he said. 'I suppose someone has stolen it. No doubt some low baron is smoking it this very moment.'

'Never mind,' Maltravers said. 'Everything will be all right when we get to Broadacres.'

He went close to where the Marquis was sitting and said something that Blore-Smith could not hear. His words seemed to have a good effect on M. de la Tour d'Espagne, who brightened up and even went so far as to supervise the latter part of his packing. When he had left the room Maltravers said:

189

'He'll be all right when he gets to the country. I'm afraid he's in a rather difficult mood now.'

'Yes.'

'I'm rather interested to see Mendie's reactions to him.'

'When will she meet him?'

'I thought we might look in on her on the way down,' Maltravers said. 'We owe her an explanation, you know. Yourself, especially.'

'But——'

Blore-Smith found difficulty in expressing how little this idea appealed to him. Maltravers said:

'Oh, don't be afraid that there will be any sort of awkwardness. Mendie is much too sensible for that. Anyway, Gaston will make a very good foil to distract her attention from ourselves.'

A short time later Blore-Smith found himself sitting beside Chipchase at the back of the car while they drove through south London. The Marquis sat beside Maltravers, and Blore-Smith could hear him explaining the plans he had for the time when he owned his tandem bicycle.

'Is this the place?' Maltravers said.

The car was drawn up in front of a gate. Beyond stood a black-and-white cottage with a thatched roof. The cottage was set back at some distance from the road and it leaned picturesquely sideways.

'This is it,' Blore-Smith said.

Maltravers, Chipchase and M. de la Tour d'Espagne set off up the crazy pavement. Blore-Smith lagged behind a little, as he was not anxious to face Mrs. Mendoza. Maltravers opened the front door and they went in. There was no sign of life.

'Mendie!' Maltravers shouted.

From upstairs a man's voice said: 'Who's that?'

Maltravers did not answer. He sat down in one of the chairs and began to glance through some snapshots that were lying on the table. A few moments later someone came heavily down the stairs. Maltravers looked up.

'Hullo?' he said.

It was Scrubb, the medical student. He was in his shirt-sleeves and covered in sweat and dirt.

'Oh, it's you all, is it?' Scrubb said.

'Yes,' said Maltravers. 'It's us. Where is Mendie?'

Scrubb said: 'She's in the garden. I'm helping her to get moved in. It's a bit of a business. There's a bricked-up fireplace upstairs. I'm opening it up.'

'In that case,' Maltravers said, 'we mustn't disturb you. We will go out in the garden and look for her. Come along.'

The others followed him out of the door and round to the back of the cottage. At the far end of the garden Blore-Smith saw Mrs. Mendoza. Wearing a bathing-dress, she was lying on a rug reading a book. When she saw them she shouted with surprise and came to meet them.

'This is a shock,' she said.

She kissed Maltravers and Chipchase. To Blore-Smith's relief she kissed him too, quite automatically, but without any sign of resentment. Maltravers said:

'This is Monsieur de la Tour d'Espagne. I expect you've both heard a lot about one another even if you haven't met before.'

'Why, of course we have,' Mrs. Mendoza said as she took the Marquis by the hand.

'We are on our way to Schlumbermayer's,' Maltravers said, 'to begin on the film right away. We were hoping we might be lucky enough to get your co-operation.'

'But, my dear, you know I'd simply adore to take part in a film.'

'I too hope for a small part,' said the Marquis, who seemed to have momentarily conquered his obsessions.

He put his head a little on one side and surveyed Mrs. Mendoza. Mrs. Mendoza smiled prettily.

'I shall be noises off,' she said.

The Marquis said: 'I could do that work too.'

'We'll do noises off together, then,' said Mrs. Mendoza.

It was clear that M. de la Tour d'Espagne had made a good impression on her.

Chipchase said: 'What is—I believe his name is *Scrubb*—doing here? I ought to warn you that when we arrived he appeared to be pulling the cottage down brick by brick. Is it your wish that he should do that?'

Mrs. Mendoza laughed and said:

'That's O.K. He will come in very useful looking after this place when I am over at Broadacres.'

'Yes. He can do that. But I should lock everything up if I were you.'

'Don't be horrible. Scrubby has been very kind.'

Mrs. Mendoza turned to Blore-Smith.

'I sent Scrubb a wire after I heard from you,' she said in a tone that gave warning that things were blowing up for a row. 'You didn't suppose I could move in here without any help, did you? You haven't told me anything about that yet.'

Maltravers took her by the arm.

'My dear Mendie,' he said, 'all that was entirely our fault. Entirely. We take all blame. We practically kidnapped him.'

Mrs. Mendoza laughed again. She was in a good mood that afternoon.

'I suppose I mustn't grumble, then,' she said.

Blore-Smith was much relieved when she said this. He knew that the subject of his telegram was bound to be raised sooner or later. He had in fact felt very guilty about the whole matter. Now everything seemed to have passed off all right. Mrs. Mendoza turned to the Marquis. She pointed to Maltravers and Chipchase.

'Aren't these two awful?' she said.

The Marquis made a sweeping movement with his hands.

'Incorrigible,' he said, rolling the r's somewhat deliberately.

'And now what about some tea?' Mrs. Mendoza said. 'I'll tell Scrubb to make some.'

'I'll come with you,' Chipchase said, 'to see that he does what he's told.'

As they walked across the lawn Mrs. Mendoza said:

'Who is the Frenchman?'

'Gaston de la Tour d'Espagne. You must have heard of him. He's a friend of Pauline Borodino's. Schlumbermayer wants to buy the contents of his château. That's why he's over here now.'

'Is he married?'

'He's had at least three wives in his time. Whether or not he has one at the moment I can't say.'

'I'm mad about him.'

'I'm not surprised.'

'I suppose he has every vice?'

'Naturally.'

Mrs. Mendoza sighed and they entered the cottage. Scrubb could be heard floundering about in the room above them. Mrs. Mendoza shouted:

'Scrubb, darling, come down and put the kettle on, will you? And get some cups and saucers out of the pantry. We'll have tea in the garden.'

Some muffled reply came from above and Mrs. Mendoza said:

'Well, be quick. We're all thirsty.'

She sat down.

'When do you want me to come over to Broadacres?' she said. 'Tonight with all of you?'

'We hoped you might be able to manage that.'

'And Scrubby can look after this place for a bit.'

'How long have you taken it for?'

'Only three months.'

Chipchase said: 'I don't want to lecture you, but it must be understood that if you come to Broadacres you are not to take our hero away again.'

Mrs. Mendoza said: 'I know, I know. I was very silly. But it brought its own punishment, as you must see for yourself by now. It won't occur again. I can promise you that.'

'In that case it looks as if we should all have a very pleasant and interesting time.'

'Does Schlumbermayer know that I am coming?'

'He seemed most anxious that you should be taking a part in the proceedings.'

'Is Sarah there?'

'She may be arriving later.'

Scrubb came down the stairs and into the room.

'What was that you shouted?' he said.

'I asked you to get the tea,' Mrs. Mendoza said. 'Don't be all night. And I shall be leaving here this evening for a day or two. Will you hold the fort?'

'But look here, I say——'

Mrs. Mendoza said: 'Now don't make a lot of silly fuss. You told me yourself you wanted a week or two in the country where you could read your medical books without being disturbed. Now I'm going to give you an opportunity to get some real work done.'

'I don't want to be left here alone.'

'We'll come over and see you. Don't worry. It will only be for a day or two.'

Scrubb disappeared into the kitchen, grumbling to himself. Mrs. Mendoza said:

'Aren't men extraordinary?'

'They are very odd,' said Chipchase.

# 6

WHEN Commander Venables came into the Long Bar he had had a depressing morning trying to clear up the mess at *la cattleya*. The flower-shop was in the hands of the bailiffs and the charwoman said that when last seen Mrs. Mendoza was driving away in a car with Mr. Scrubb, who had taken a suitcase with him. She gave Commander Venables the address that Scrubb had left for the forwarding of letters, but she was unable to tell him whether or not Mrs. Mendoza was staying in the same place. From something that Scrubb had said, this seemed probable. Commander Venables thanked her and went away. He was in need of refreshment.

Inglethorne was already in the Long Bar when Commander Venables arrived. Unlike Commander Venables, Inglethorne was in the best of tempers. He had just signed a satisfactory contract and he had already had one or two on the strength of it. He gripped Commander Venables by the hand and, although he was a much smaller man, threw an arm round his shoulder and led him to the bar. Commander Venables put up no opposition. He needed sympathy. Inglethorne said:

'And how's the little lady we met with you in Berlin? Mrs. Mendoza. You don't meet girls like that growing on every rose-bush.'

Commander Venables put his drink back and ordered the same again. Then he took a deep breath.

'Well . . .' he said.

Inglethorne, suddenly switching over to a different sort of acting, said hoarsely:

'Tell me, man. Don't keep me in suspense.'

Commander Venables was taken by surprise. He was not used to actors. He felt Inglethorne's fingers digging into his arm.

'It's like this,' he said.

Inglethorne was a good listener. He was accustomed to practise facial expressions when other people were talking, and in his disquiet at the series of studies in physiognomy that Inglethorne called up, ranging from nauseated ennui to uncontrollable passion, Commander Venables said more than he intended. He told the whole story, or as much as he knew of it. It took some time.

'And now she seems to be living in the country with a medical student.'

'Do you know him?' Inglethorne said.

'He's been her lodger for ages.'

'But, my dear old boy,' said Inglethorne. 'My dear old boy! There's probably nothing in it at all. Positively nothing. After all, why should she have waited until now? Take my advice and go down and see her as soon as possible.'

The possibility of a platonic relationship between Mrs. Mendoza and Scrubb seemed to have escaped Commander Venables's consideration.

'But she surely wouldn't do that,' he said.

'Why not?'

'Well, what does she want to take him for, then?'

'To help her get moved in perhaps.'

Commander Venables looked uncertain. Inglethorne took two steps back and looked down into his open palm with the gesture of one who has just received a tip and verifies the amount. He said:

> *'O, beware, my lord, of jealousy;*
> *It is the green-eyed monster, which doth mock*
> *The meat it feeds on: that cuckold lives in bliss*
> *Who, certain of his fate, loves not his wronger;*
> *But, O, what damned minutes tells he o'er*
> *Who dotes, yet doubts, suspects, yet strongly loves!'*

'So you think——'

> *'Poor and content is rich,'* said Inglethorne, *'and rich enough;*
> *But riches fineless is as poor as winter*
> *To him that ever fears he shall be poor:*
> *Good heaven, the souls of all my tribe defend*
> *From jealousy!'*

Having said this, Inglethorne pulled his hat farther down over his eyes, put his hands in his pockets and hunched his shoulders. It was a sign that he had moved on from his Shakespearean role.

'But what is the best way to tackle the situation?'

'Have you got a car?' Inglethorne said.

Commander Venables nodded. Inglethorne said:

'Buzz down to see her with a little present tomorrow. Something unexpected. Caviare and some fizz. Offer her that. She won't refuse.'

Commander Venables was not a demonstrative man, but he could not prevent himself from banging with his fist on the bar so that he nearly upset a bottle of tonic water belonging to the young motor salesman next to him.

'I believe you're right, Inglethorne,' he said.

'Of course I am, old boy,' said Inglethorne. 'I should start at once. Have another before you go.'

It was still early afternoon when Commander Venables, driving a battered two-seater from which the hood had been removed some years before, approached the white cottage. On the seat beside him was a basket containing two magnums of champagne, a pot of caviare, some *foie gras,* and a tin of biscuits. Some enquiry was necessary before he found his way, and after being several times misdirected a woman pointed to where it could be seen through the trees.

'Young fellow lives there by himself,' she said.

Commander Venables grunted and drove on. When he reached the gate he stopped the car and looked about for a few minutes to see if there was any sign of Mrs. Mendoza in the front garden. No one seemed to be about, so he took his basket and went up the crazy pavement. The front door was ajar. Commander Venables knocked sharply. He heard someone inside walking across the stone floor. The door was pulled open.

At first, because he had several days' growth of beard, Commander Venables did not recognise Scrubb. He thought it was the boy who cleaned the boots or looked after the garden.

'Is Mrs Mendoza in?' he said.

After he had said this he saw that it was Scrubb, and added:

'Where's Mendie? Didn't recognise you for the moment. I brought her down a little present.'

Scrubb took the basket. He said:

'Is this food?'

'Just a few odds and ends.'

Without asking Commander Venables's permission Scrubb took a knife and began to prise open the biscuit tin. He said:

'The last I saw of Mendie was a week ago. She went off

to do this film. I've been here with no food except what I could get on tick, which wasn't much; no money, and no way of getting away. What do you think of that?'

Commander Venables did not answer. He watched Scrubb take a handful of biscuits and put them in his mouth. Scrubb said:

'She asks me to come down here for a couple of days to help her move in and says that she'll motor me back to London, and then what happens? She just goes off to let me starve to death.'

'But didn't she say when she was coming back?'

'Of course she said she was coming back the next day. A fat lot of good it does her saying that. Besides, she's gone off with Maltravers and Chipchase and that crowd, so there's precious little likelihood that any of us will see her for some time.'

'But where's she gone to?'

'To Schlumbermayer's.'

'Who is Schlumbermayer?'

Scrubb had his mouth full and he made a disagreeable sound to indicate his contempt for Commander Venables's ignorance. Commander Venables said:

'But did she come down here to live by herself?'

'Live by herself? She came down here to live with Blore-Smith.'

'Blore-Smith?'

'The little chap she came back from Germany with.'

Although Scrubb was interested primarily in his own troubles, something about Commander Venables's face made him say:

'Why, didn't you know?'

'That—little——'

Commander Venables made no attempt to express in words the mental agitation that assailed him. He went to the basket and, taking out one of the magnums of champagne, said:

'Have you got a glass?'

'What's that? Bubbly?' Scrubb said. 'There are only tumblers, but they will do.'

He hurried to the kitchen and came back with the glasses just as Commander Venables drew the cork. Commander Venables poured out two full tumblers and sat down.

'Where does this blighter live?' he said. 'Where Mendie's gone?'

'About thirty miles from here.'

'Are they all there?'

'All who?'

'Maltravers and Chipchase and Blore-Smith. All that gang?'

'Of course they are. They're doing this film, I tell you.'

'I don't give a damn whether they're doing a film or not,' Commander Venables said. 'I propose to go over there.'

'But look here,' said Scrubb. 'You can't leave me here. Now you've arrived you must take me back.'

'You can come with me if you like.'

'I certainly do like. I don't want to stay here any longer with the baker threatening non-delivery every day and no prospect of ever seeing Mendie again.'

Commander Venables poured himself out another glass of champagne and Scrubb held out his own tumbler. He was already flushed from the effect of the wine. He said:

'Wait half a minute and I'll put my pyjamas and toothbrush into a suitcase, and then we'll go anywhere you like so long as we get away from here.'

'Right.'

When Scrubb came downstairs again he found that Commander Venables had opened the second magnum.

'What about having some caviare with it?' Scrubb said.

'Any damn thing you like.'

By the time they set out for Schlumbermayer's there was little left of the original contents of the basket that had been intended as a present for Mrs. Mendoza.

The company at Broadacres were sitting and lying in various positions on the lawn in front of the house. They consisted of Blore-Smith, Maltravers, Chipchase, Schlumbermayer, Mrs. Mendoza, M. de la Tour d'Espagne, and Sarah. Blore-Smith sat a little apart from the rest, watching Mrs. Mendoza and the Marquis, who lay on the same rug, holding hands. A camera, resting in a tripod, stood at some distance from the group. Maltravers, who was sitting in a deck-chair, held a sheaf of papers in his hand. On these he was making notes with a blue pencil. Without looking up, he said:

'As regards the individual studies we now seem to have a fairly comprehensive series of shots, taken both when the subject was unaware that he or she was being photographed and also when aware that this was happening.'

Turning to Schlumbermayer, he said:

'There are some specially good ones of you.'

Schlumbermayer rubbed his nose. He said:

'And so what?'

Maltravers put down the papers on the grass beside him.

'We must now wait for things to happen,' he said. 'My experience tells me that usually one does not have to wait long.'

He lit a cigarette and lay back in his chair. Sarah said:

'Here's someone coming to pay a call.'

She pointed to a small dreadnought-grey car which had appeared from among the trees at the beginning of the drive and was now skirting the wide stretch of grass that lay fenced off on the farther side of the gravel. As it came nearer it was noticeable that the car had no hood and that both of the men who sat inside it were red in the face. Chipchase said:

'Do you know, for a moment I thought one of them was the Commodore.'

Maltravers shaded his eyes.

'You were right,' he said. 'It is the Commodore.'

'And the other is Scrubb,' said Sarah.

Chipchase said: 'Scrubb? What have we done to deserve him? Anyway, what does either of them want here?'

'Heaven knows,' Maltravers said. 'However, they will make a very suitable addition to our little group of behaviour-actors. Keep your eye on the camera for developments.'

'Mendie,' Chipchase said. 'Two friends of yours are arriving by car. If the engine holds out they will be here quite soon.'

Mrs. Mendoza rolled over on the rug without loosening her grasp of the Marquis's hand. She said:

'What's all that?'

'The Commodore and Scrubb are chugging up the drive.'

'Nonsense!'

Mrs. Mendoza sat upright. Commander Venables and Scrubb moved painfully forward. At last there was a sound of squeaking brakes and the small car stopped. Without bothering to open the door Commander Venables threw his leg over the side of the car and climbed out. He came slowly towards them across the grass. Scrubb followed him. Both of them had a high colour. Maltravers nudged Chipchase and jerked his head in the direction of the camera. Then he jumped up and said:

'Hullo, Captain Venables. Why haven't you come to see us before?'

Chipchase crawled hurriedly in the direction of the camera.

Commander Venables took no notice of Maltravers. He went straight to Mrs. Mendoza. Turning away from the group Maltravers said:

'Have you got your distance?'

'Half a minute,' said Chipchase. 'Now I have.'

Mrs. Mendoza said: 'My dear Hugo, this is a great surprise. You aren't wearing very country clothes, though, are you?'

'Never mind about my clothes,' Commander Venables said. 'Come here.'

He took her by the wrist and pulled her up from ground. Mrs. Mendoza cried out at the violence with which he did this.

'Shoot!' said Maltravers.

'O.K.' said Chipchase.

The noise of the camera was lost in Mrs. Mendoza's flow of protest. Additionally so on account of the vibrations from an aeroplane that was passing in the sky above them. Mrs. Mendoza said:

'Are you drunk, Hugo?'

'No, I'm not drunk,' Commander Venables said, still holding her tightly by the wrist. 'I've just come down to say a few words about the way you've behaved to me, and not to me only. What about that damned flower-shop of yours with the brokers in? What about the way you treated me in Berlin? What about that filthy little brute Herman and all the little brutes before him, and after him too? What about this chap you left to starve to death at your cottage? What about all your friends? All these? They are your friends, aren't they?'

By this time Commander Venables's voice was like a foghorn. The extreme passion of his rage was infectious and Blore-Smith felt himself trembling all over while small electric shocks ran up and down his arms. Scrubb, paralysed by what he saw taking place, stood with his hands in his pockets and his mouth open. Mrs. Mendoza snatched her hand away. She said:

'Are you mad?'

At this point Blore-Smith felt his arm seized so tightly that he could not help gasping with pain. It was M. de la Tour d'Espagne who held him. The Marquis had risen to his hands and knees, and said in a hoarse voice, close to Blore-Smith's ear:

'Introduce me!'

'Who to?'

'To this man!'

'To Commander Venables?'

'Yes, yes. Quickly!'

'But——'

The pain caused by the Marquis's fingers in the fleshy part of his arm was so intense that in order to do anything to allay it Blore-Smith scrambled to his feet. The Marquis followed him quickly. Sweating with fear, Blore-Smith said:

'Oh, Commander Venables, this is the Marquis de la Tour d'Espagne.'

Commander Venables swivelled round and looked at the Marquis, who was standing stiffly to attention. From him Commander Venables turned his eyes again to Blore-Smith. As he did this the Marquis bowed smartly and took two little steps forward which brought him so close to Commander Venables that their noses almost touched.

'Sir,' he said.

Commander Venables shied away his face, like an angry horse. He said:

'And what can I do for you?'

'You must behave more politely,' the Marquis said, in a very quiet voice.

There was a stillness as before an earthquake, broken only by the ticking of the camera and the more insistent buzzings of the aeroplane that was now circling above the house. Mrs. Mendoza said:

'Don't take any notice of him, Gaston. He must have been drinking. It's not altogether his fault, because he has a very weak head.'

Commander Venables looked at M. de la Tour d'Espagne for some seconds.

'Go to hell,' he said, also very quietly.

M. de la Tour d'Espagne smiled. He began to fumble in his breast pocket. From here he took a notecase and, after a short search, he found a visiting-card. He handed this to Commander Venables.

'If you will give me your address,' he said, 'I will instruct my seconds to call on you. Choice of weapons will of course be with you.'

Commander Venables put his hands in his pockets and stared into M. de la Tour d'Espagne's face. He pursed his lips. It seemed that he found this particular situation unexpected. He had taken the card in his hand and now he examined it without enthusiasm. The Marquis looked round at the others. Blore-Smith avoided his eye in case the Marquis should fix on him as a desirable second. Commander Venables breathed heavily. At last he said:

'You had better get out. We don't fight duels in England.'

He tore the card into four pieces and dropped them on the grass. M. de la Tour d'Espagne's face began to twitch in a way that Blore-Smith could now recognise as a warning of trouble in the offing. He began to clasp and unclasp his hands in front of him. His cheeks became a shade less grey than was usual with him. He said:

'The blood——'

He was interrupted by Sarah.

'Look!' she said. 'Why, an aeroplane is coming down in the big field!'

Schlumbermayer now got up from the pile of cushions from which he had been watching matters. He took out his spectacles and put them on. He said:

'What do they mean by coming down here? It's private property.'

Maltravers turned again to Chipchase. He said:

'Cut. New material.'

'Just a moment,' Chipchase said.

He shifted round the camera. The aeroplane bumped along the length of the field, turned, and came to a standstill. For a time nothing happened and then a short figure climbed out. It was a man, and he turned and helped another passenger to the ground. The second arrival was swathed in coats and scarves. Some of these were removed and a woman was revealed. She took the man's arm and both began to walk away from the aeroplane in the direction of the house. Schlumbermayer said:

'Who do you suppose these are?'

He advanced a few steps to meet them. Maltravers said:

'One of them is remarkably like Reggie Frott.'

'And if I'm not mistaken,' said Schlumbermayer, 'the other is the Duchesse de Borodino.'

'What? Pauline?'

In the excitement M. de la Tour d'Espagne seemed to have forgotten about the duel. Commander Venables, too, seemed cowed and half ashamed of his earlier fury. Maltravers said:

'Don't miss them as they climb over the railings, Oliver.'

Reggie Frott and the Duchesse de Borodino approached. Schlumbermayer, by way of greeting, made some uneasy passes with his hands in their direction. Reggie Frott waved him aside.

'It's Gaston we've come to see,' he said. 'I'll talk to you later, old boy. Business first.'

Blore-Smith found himself shaking hands with the Duchesse de Borodino. As usual she was beaming and telling everybody what an amusing time they had had.

'It's an air-taxi,' she said. 'We thought it was going to come down in the middle of the Channel.'

Reggie Frott took M. de la Tour d'Espagne by the arm.

'Gaston, *mon vieux*,' he said, 'I'm acting as an agent for Lazarus Kolf. He wants to buy all your junk. Everything. The whole doings, lock, stock, and barrel. It's the best offer you're ever likely to get. House, pictures, tapestry, furniture, *droit de seigneur*. The whole bag of tricks.'

Reggie took a sheet of paper from his pocket and began to unscrew the top of his fountain-pen.

'Why not sign the preliminary thing at once?' he said. 'It's not binding in any way except that it gives Kolf a fortnight's option. Why, we've been hunting all over Europe for you.'

Schlumbermayer came hurrying forward.

'What's all this, Frott,' he said. 'You haven't come here to try to——'

'Just the odd spot of business,' Reggie Frott said. 'Nothing to get excited about.'

The Marquis said: 'Is it ready money?'

'If you come back to Paris you can walk straight into Kolf's office and get the cheque tonight. He's always there until past nine o'clock at night.'

'Look here,' said Schlumbermayer. 'What do you want butting in like this? Gaston and I are fixing up a deal——'

'Why not go back in our air-taxi, Gaston?' Reggie Frott said. 'Pauline and I are on our way to London. I thought that if I found you here I could fix things up satisfactorily, and we have ordered a car to come down from London and pick us up here. It should arrive at any minute now. In fact I expect it is already out at the back, waiting.'

M. de la Tour d'Espagne put his hand to his forehead. He seemed to be making a colossal effort to come to a decision. Then he said:

'I go back at once in your plane.'

He turned to Mrs. Mendoza.

'*Tu viens, chérie?*' he said.

Mrs. Mendoza prided herself on her French.

'*Tout de suite?*' she said.

'*Pourquoi pas?*' said the Marquis.

He took her by the hand and they began to run towards the big field. At first Commander Venables, himself no French scholar, did not realise what was on foot. Even so he was the first of the others to take action. He began to run after them. His speed was remarkable for a man of his age and build. By the time M. de la Tour d'Espagne and Mrs. Mendoza had reached the railings he was close behind them. Mrs. Mendoza climbed over. The Marquis turned and, lowering his head, butted Commander Venables in the wind, just as he arrived. The impact was considerable owing to the exertion of Commander Venables himself. Commander Venables went down. The Marquis vaulted the rail and caught up Mrs. Mendoza. Both of them hurried on towards the aeroplane. Commander Venables lay on the grass. Maltravers said:

'That's an apache trick.'

All this happened so quickly that Blore-Smith was aware of little more than a feeling of terror and nausea that had now become unbearable. All he could remember were Reggie Frott's words about a car waiting at the back of the house. He began to edge away in the direction of the front door. His things would not take long to throw into a bag. As he went he heard Schlumbermayer, shaking with rage, say: 'You'll be sorry for this, Frott'; and Maltravers shouting, 'Come on, don't miss anything'; while Chipchase again replied, 'O.K.'

Carrying his suitcase, Blore-Smith stumbled down the back stairs and went along the passage and out into the stable-yard. A large saloon car, with a uniformed chauffeur, was waiting there. The chauffeur touched his cap and took the suitcase from Blore-Smith. He said:

'And the lady, sir?'

'She won't be coming,' Blore-Smith said. 'I'm a bit late myself, so drive to London as soon possible.'

'Very good, sir.'

'And leave here by the back way.'

'Yes, sir.'

As they went out of the gate Blore-Smith, looking through the window, saw an aeroplane mounting towards the clouds. He lay back in the seat. The car drove on, gathering speed. It was not long before they entered the outskirts of London.

'What address, sir?' said the chauffeur.

'Ebury Street.'

It was the only home he knew, and he had decided to throw himself on Mrs. Pinkus's mercy. Later, when they had reached their destination, the chauffeur said.

'It's down to the Duchess's account, isn't it, sir?'

'Yes,' said Blore-Smith.

He fumbled in his pocket, thinking that he ought to give the man a tip, but as he seemed to have only a few coppers there he just said, 'Good afternoon,' and, picking up his suitcase, walked towards the house.

Mrs. Pinkus herself opened the door. She heard all that Blore-Smith had to say. Then she waited for a time, feeling abstractedly her back hair. She said:

'You'll be quite alone this time?'

'Quite alone,' Blore-Smith said.

'Because——'

'Yes, yes,' said Blore-Smith. 'I know. I shall be quite alone this time and I shall remain quite alone.'

'Well,' Mrs. Pinkus said, 'the old accommodation is free. But I've had to raise my terms. They would be five shillings a week more than you were paying before.'

'All right. I'll take them on again.'

'In that case,' Mrs. Pinkus said, 'you'll find everything much as before. You know when you went away so sudden you never told the telephone you were leaving nor the gas neither.'

When Blore-Smith left her in the hall, she was still feeling her heavily embankmented hair as if she feared that the whole affair might come away from its moorings.

Blore-Smith spent the next few days trying to make plans for going abroad. That seemed the best thing to do. He went to several travel agencies, but he experienced his former inability to take action, now that the excitement of escaping from Broadacres was past. And then one evening after tea there was a knock on his door.

'Come in,' said Blore-Smith.

It was Maltravers and Chipchase. Blore-Smith got up quickly from his chair.

'What do you want?' he said.

'We came round to see you,' Maltravers said.

'Well, I don't want to see either of you.'

'That is very unfriendly of you. Besides you owe some sort of an explanation with regard to the virtual theft of a car.'

'I took it to get away from you.'

'You caused a lot of inconvenience.'

'I don't care.'

'That is a matter of taste. Meanwhile someone else has had to pay for your journey. In short there is an account to settle.'

'It's been the same all the way along,' Blore-Smith said. 'You've just been trying to get money out of me.'

'But, good heavens,' Maltravers said, 'whoever suggested that we were doing anything else? We've got to live. Do you expect two ambitious men to devote their whole time to looking after you just for your *beaux yeux*? You seem to have exchanged your inferiority complex for paranoia.'

'The whole of this talk about psychology is a ramp. You've just used it as a way to swindle me.'

'It seems nevertheless to have had a very formative effect on your character. You don't suggest, do you, that you would have had the courage to talk to me like this when we first met?'

'You hadn't tried your tricks on me then.'

'And very apparent it was. Why, you couldn't say boo to a goose when I first saw you.'

'Anyway,' said Blore-Smith, who had begun to shake violently, 'I'm through with you now—and you.'

Maltravers slowly bowed but said nothing. Chipchase walked across to the sideboard and began to mix himself a drink.

'Ever since I met you,' Blore-Smith said, 'my life has been nothing but worry and strain. I haven't known what peace of mind means.'

'Whose fault is that?' Maltravers said, putting his hat on and sitting on the edge of the table.

'It's your fault. Both your faults. That's what I am complaining about.'

Maltravers said:

'I could tell you weren't pleased about something. But surely the fact that you worry too much is largely your own fault. Or I prefer to say that it is something that time and a good deal of application may cure. I cannot see that either of us is to be blamed for that.'

'It is you who brought me into touch with all the people who cause me to worry. All the beastly people in this film, for instance.'

'I thought you wanted to meet a few people? You complained that your acquaintance was so limited when first we met and discussed such matters.'

'I didn't know the dregs I know now.'

'You showed every sign of wanting to.'

'I didn't want to be dragged down as you've dragged me down.'

'It would have been hard work dragging you lower than the niche you were occupying when we found you,' Chipchase said, finishing his drink and replacing the glass on the sideboard. 'You must admit that. In fact the obscurity would soon have become so inspissated that you would almost certainly have become completely lost sight of.'

'At least I wasn't paying away all my income to you and your sharks.'

'Come, come,' said Chipchase. 'Please remember that there is such a thing as slander and that the law in this country is for rich and poor alike. Beware the fury of a patient man.'

Blore-Smith's teeth began to chatter. He had lost all control of himself and could no longer speak.

'Mind you,' said Chipchase, 'it would be with real reluctance that I should put matters in the hands of my solicitor.'

Maltravers swung his legs up on to the table and turned round, and over, so that he lay along it, supporting his chin on his hands.

'But what is really the matter?' he said. 'When we met you your life was of a dullness so intolerable that you thought of suicide. You told me so. I repeat your very words. We take you in hand and in the space of a few months you are in the thick of everything. Love affairs. Business dealings of the most varied kind. Travel. Strange company. Adventure. What else do you want? What else do you imagine life has to offer? I admit that it has cost you some money, but, after all, the money is no good unless you use it for something. In your case you didn't even keep it in gold on the premises and count it every night. Even that would have been more fun than you got out of it by your own efforts.'

'Well, I want to be left alone now.'

'Alone,' said Maltravers, 'is precisely the state in which you are going to be left. It was to tell you this that we came round tonight.'

'Have you found some other fool to make money out of?'

'You have the coarsest way of putting things,' Maltravers said, 'but in a sense, yes. I have. We both have, in fact. We are crossing the Atlantic at the end of next week.'

'Who are you going to sponge on there?'

'On Hollywood, it may interest you to hear.'

'Both of you?'

'No,' said Chipchase. 'I am giving a course of lectures on sub-normal psychology. I shall find some of my notes on your own behaviour of great use for purposes of illustration.'

'Then I am really going to see the last of you?'

In spite of himself Blore-Smith allowed his voice to sound apprehensive. He had been prepared for a row but hardly for something so final as this.

'And what are your plans, may one enquire?' said Maltravers.

'I shall lead my own life again.'

'I see.'

'Not the life foisted on me by you two. Something very different.'

214

'I can imagine that.'

'The real thing,' said Blore-Smith, rather desperately.

'If,' said Chipchase, 'you imagine that the Real Thing is ever going to be widely different from what you have already experienced, I fear that you may be disappointed. However——'

'I'll risk that,' Blore-Smith said.

'In that case,' Maltravers said, 'we will take up no more of your valuable time. There are, however, a few items here.'

He handed Blore-Smith a sheaf of bills. Chipchase said: 'And the tail-end of my own account.'

Blore-Smith took the pieces of paper hurriedly. For a moment it looked as if he were going to tear them up. Then he turned to his desk and, still standing, he wrote out a cheque and handed it over.

'Thank you,' said Chipchase, 'and good-bye.'

'Before we part, a small token of our regard,' Maltravers said. He handed Blore-Smith an envelope. 'Should you want us we shall be at Broadacres for the next few days. Poor Schlumbermayer needs companionship. He has had a shock.'

They went through the door, leaving Blore-Smith standing in the middle of the room holding the envelope in his hand. Blore-Smith heard the front door slam. He tore open the envelope. Inside was a snapshot of Maltravers and Chipchase sitting on either side of one of the urns in the garden at Broadacres. Blore-Smith looked at it for a long time. Then he threw it in the waste-paper basket.

Later, he picked it out of the waste-paper basket and propped it up on the mantelpiece. After that he sat down on the hard chair and looked out of the window. It had begun to rain and small drops of water were running down the glass.

When the telephone bell rang nearly an hour later he was

215

still sitting there, in the same position. He took up the receiver.

'Hullo?'

'Is Mr. Blore-Smith there?'

The voice seemed familiar. It recalled faintly some out-of-the-way experience.

'Who is that speaking?'

'This is Colonel Teape.'

'Oh—I see—yes. This is me speaking.'

'What a piece of luck finding you,' Colonel Teape said. 'You remember me? I so hope you do.'

'Why yes—of course.'

'How frightfully clever of you.'

'We have met—several times.'

'Yes,' said Colonel Teape. 'We have.'

In the distance he laughed a little.

'How's life been treating you?' he said.

'Oh, I don't know. Nothing very exciting really.'

'A bit bored?'

'Oh well, I don't know——'

'Oh yes, you are. I can tell at once. Now will you do something for me? Something that will please me a lot?'

Blore-Smith was aware of a sinking feeling inside him.

'What?' he said, trying to prevent his voice from trembling.

'I've taken a little house in the south of France—not far from St. Tropez, as a matter of fact. Just for the summer. I want you to come and stay with me there.'

'Why——?'

'Will you come? It would be so delightful.'

'St. Tropez?' said Blore-Smith. 'I—— Look here, do you mind if I write to you about it. I think——'

'I don't mind if you write and tell me that you can come,'

Colonel Teape said. 'But if you were naughty enough to tell me that you couldn't, I should be very cross indeed.'

'I must say,' said Chipchase, cutting the cards to Sarah Maltravers, 'I think it was very kind of Pauline and Reggie Frott to take Scrubb back with them to London. I feel a great sense of relief now that he has gone.'

Sarah began to deal. She said:

'Anybody else but Pauline would have made a fuss about the car being taken like that. Still, I suppose she can perfectly well afford to ring up and order another one when that sort of thing happens.'

'It's a jackpot,' Schlumbermayer said.

Commander Venables, who was looking all the better for his stay in the country, said:

'I think our host ought to be congratulated too. On his good-nature in letting me stay here.'

'Oh, he's the best-natured man in the world,' Chipchase said, 'even though he hasn't ante-ed yet. Personally I can't open.'

Schlumbermayer pushed two chips forward. He said:

'Nor can I.'

'Peter?' Sarah said.

Maltravers sat without speaking, brooding over his cards. He said:

'You know, I've been thinking about Blore-Smith. What is he going to make of his life?'

'Can you open?'

'Yes. I'll open for two,' Maltravers said. 'And please don't be so aggressive when you speak to me. As I have said before, I think that young man made a grave mistake.'

'I'll come in,' said Commander Venables.

'So will I,' Sarah and Chipchase said at the same moment.

Schlumbermayer took some minutes to decide. At last, unwillingly, he thrust two more chips forward. Sarah dealt out the cards. Schlumbermayer said:

'I don't see how I can expect to win. Luck goes in waves and I haven't had any now for two years.'

'You'd better come out to America with us,' Maltravers said, 'and try your hand there.'

He opened the betting with two. Commander Venables said:

'I'll see that. I wish it was America I was going to and not Basra.'

Sarah said: 'I'll raise you one.'

'I'll see you,' Chipchase said.

Schlumbermayer frowned horribly and fiddled with his spectacles.

Chipchase said: 'I'm not sure that I really want to go to America now that it is all fixed. I'm trying to arrange for Caroline to come as my secretary with all expenses paid, but there seems to be some hitch. People seem to take a malicious pleasure in putting difficulties in one's way.'

With an effort, Schlumbermayer said: 'I'll raise that two.'

Maltravers began to count the chips on the table. He pushed two piles of his own counters forward.

'Raise you the pool,' he said.

Commander Venables put down his cards heavily and gave a deep sigh.

'I'm away,' Sarah said.

'So am I,' said Chipchase.

Again Schlumbermayer sat wrapped in thought. Commander Venables said:

'You know, there I shall be with a few other white men, all talking of tiffin and *chota-hazri* and sighing for Piccadilly, and, do you know, I shan't have a word to say to them? It will be awful to feel different. After all, one's the same breed. But somehow when you've been through a good deal and you find yourself a few thousand miles from civilisation, whether it's on land or on sea, and you've had dinner —it will be at half-past six in those parts—and you're sitting there in your evening clothes—or rather your pyjamas, which is what you change into in the tropics—you look up at those stars and you can't help developing a sort of philosophy of life.'

Schlumbermayer threw in his hand. Maltravers began to rake the kitty towards him. Schlumbermayer said:

'Let's see your openers.'

Maltravers picked up his cards and, extracting two knaves, flicked them across the table.